Tanka Socie͏̈

Founc͏̈

Official Website: www.tankasocietyofamerica.org

Ribbons **Editor:** Susan Weaver
127 N. 10th St., Allentown, PA 18102; RibbonsEditor@gmail.com

Tanka Hangout Editor: Ken Slaughter
24 Briarwood Circle, Worcester, MA 01606; tsahangout@outlook.com

Tanka Prose Editor: Liz Lanigan
38 McClure St., EVATT ACT 2617, Australia
TankaProseEditor@gmail.com

President and Webperson: Michael Dylan Welch
22230 N.E. 28th Pl., Sammamish, WA 98074-6408; welchm@aol.com

Vice President: Susan Burch
9128 Cool Hollow Terr., Hagerstown, MD 21740; sehbtree@yahoo.com

Second Vice President: Ryland Shengzhi Li
Arlington, VA; liryland+tsaboard@gmail.com

Secretary: Kathabela Wilson
439 S. Catalina Ave. #306, Pasadena, CA 91106; poetsonsite@gmail.com

Treasurer: James Won
6233 Golden West, Temple City, CA 91780; jameswon@charter.net

Cover: *Lotus and Enso: Spiritual Harmony,* mixed media, 6 x 4, by Emma Alexander Arthur, Zen Arts Studio.

Cover Design: Christine L. Villa

Submission Guidelines: See last pages of journal.

Business Address: 439 S. Catalina Ave. #306, Pasadena, CA 91106

Ribbons: **Tanka Society of America Journal**, published triannually in Winter, Spring/Summer, and Fall. All prior copyrights are retained by contributors, and full rights revert on publication. Neither the TSA, its officers, nor the *Ribbons* editors assume responsibility for the views of contributors (including TSA officers) whose work is printed in *Ribbons*.

TSA Memberships include triannual issues of the Tanka Society of America's journal, *Ribbons,* plus the members' anthology. A one-year membership costs USD: $30 USA; $35 Canada and Mexico; and $42 elsewhere. Make all checks or money orders payable to the Tanka Society of America and mail to Kathabela Wilson, TSA Secretary, 439 S. Catalina Ave. #306, Pasadena, CA 91106.

Additional copies of recent issues of *Ribbons* may be ordered from our production partner at www.amazon.com. (Payment by PayPal is available from Amazon.) For questions about payment for non-US residents, contact Kathabela Wilson by e-mail: poetsonsite@gmail.com.

ISSN: 2150-4954

Copyright © 2023 by the Tanka Society of America

RIBBONS

Spring/Summer 2023: Volume 19, Number 2

CONTENTS

The Back Cover by Susan Weaver and Marilyn Fleming, 4
Tanka Art (Tanka by David F. Noble; Art by Christine L. Villa), 5
President's Message by Michael Dylan Welch, 6
Editor's Message by Susan Weaver, 8
Tanka Hangout: Member's Choice by Elinor Pihl Huggett, 10
Tanka Hangout: Compassion, 12
Tanka Hangout's Next Theme: Tribute Poems, 31
Tanka Art by an'ya, 32
Selected Tanka, 33
Tanka Art by Barbara Kaufmann, 59
Tanka Sequences and Strings, 60
Responsive Tanka, 76
Tanka Art (Tanka by Pamela A. Babusci; Art by Dawn Robinson), 80
Tanka Prose, 81
Tanka Art by Debbie Strange, 99
Sanford Goldstein's Tanka World: Part 1—A Diary of the Emotional Changes in a Man's Life by Randy Brooks, 100
Book Reviews:
  Earthbound, **An Aerial View through a Tanka Lens** by Ginny Short, 114
  Bouquets of Migrant Tales: *wildflowers* by Ginny Short, 117
  Lifetimes in the Veins by Jenny Ward Angyal, 121
  An Ancient Tradition with a Modern Twist by Peggy Hale Bilbro, 126
News and Announcements, 130
Tanka Art by an'ya, 130
Index of Contributors, 131
Submission Guidelines, 134

The Back Cover

> white space
> between plum blossoms
> sumi-e
> the way we are close
> but not too close
>
> *Marilyn Fleming, Pewaukee, WI*

In this tanka, I notice several things. First, what's not mentioned are the color and abundant fragrance of these blooms known as *ume* in Japan, which appear in chilly weather before the cherry trees flower.

Instead, this is a monochromatic poem, and rightly so. Its first three lines concern the white space in black-ink paintings termed *sumi-e* by the Japanese. It's as much about what is not painted, as about what is. Lines one and three are appropriately spare.

Continuing on, line four introduces a link and shift with an implied comparison. Now the tanka seems to reflect on relationships —human ones—and the fine line between being "close/ but not too close." Is the poet referring to a specific partnership or speaking more generally, or both? In any case, it's a thought-provoking tanka that resonates with me. I asked Marilyn Fleming to share her perspective.

"I am speaking of the natural world," she writes, "as well as of personal relationships, whether they be spouse, children, or other family. When sowing seeds, one should keep a space between the seeds, so they have a chance to develop individually. Bushes and trees that grow too close together will diminish each other. Likewise, in our relationships, even children need their own space to develop and grow.

"And I am also tying it in with the white space on rice paper, in sumi-e painting, that is intentionally left open. For example, if painting a plum branch, I will lift the brush to leave a little space and then continue on defining the branch. This technique can enhance the branch, and/or the blossom.

"When I was first introduced to sumi-e, it made a lasting impression on me, in the way 'less is more.' It is simple and yet, because of its simplicity, it is not easy to achieve. This is somewhat like writing tanka. The words are few, but often what is left out adds to the meaning of the poem. It can suggest but not tell."

She closes with the words of Kahlil Gibran: "But let there be space in your togetherness. And let the winds of the heavens dance between you."

—Susan Weaver

rings of growth are witness
to seasons and storms—
how many branches
will this 95-year-old
be blessed to see?

David F. Noble

President's Message

On May 5, 2023, the world of tanka lost a beloved icon, Sanford Goldstein, for whom the Tanka Society of America renamed its annual tanka contest in 2015. He died at the age of ninety-seven in Niigata, Japan, in a house he'd built himself, where he had lived for the last twenty-three years with his companion, Kazuaki Wakui. Sandy was a pioneer in English-language tanka, and a translator of key twentieth century tanka texts by Ishikawa Takuboku, Akiko Yosano, and Mokichi Saitō, among others. He was a tanka mentor to countless poets, in addition to being a professor of English at Purdue University and later Keiwa College in Niigata. It is hard to imagine anyone writing tanka in English, past or present, who has not been touched by Sanford Goldstein's abiding and always nurturing influence.

The Tanka Society of America is remembering and celebrating Sanford Goldstein in several ways. The first, in this issue of *Ribbons*, is part one of a two-part essay by Randy Brooks, who was a student of Sanford's at Purdue. I had asked Randy to write this essay long before Sandy passed away, but now this premonition is an especially fitting tribute to this tanka legend. The essay's second part will appear in the next issue. In both essays you will learn a great deal more about Sandy's varied and storied career as a tanka poet, translator, and educator, and how he "spilled" his honest record of tanka for most of his adult life. Randy will also be delivering a concentrated version of his tribute at our Tanka Monday event on July 3 in Cincinnati, Ohio. In addition, Sandy will be included in the 2023 Haiku North America conference memorial reading, slated for June 30, 2023, also in Cincinnati.

Another celebration of Sanford Goldstein will take place on Zoom on August 26, 2023, at 7:00 p.m. Eastern Time, 4:00 pm Pacific Time. Watch for more details about this reading and how you can participate with favorite poems by Sandy, your own tribute tanka, and any memories you're able to share. We may also be able to present selected poems from this event on our Facebook page.

While we are saddened at Sandy's passing, we are also excited to have our special Tanka Monday conference at Cincinnati's historic Mercantile Library on July 3, immediately after this year's Haiku North America conference. Events will begin the evening before at the Netherland Plaza Hotel with readings by Mariko Kitakubo, Deborah P Kolodji, and Kozue Uzawa, plus an open-mic reading. On July 3 our speakers will include Randy Brooks, Tish Davis, Marilyn Shoemaker Hazelton, and Michael Dylan Welch, among others. We'll also have an anonymous workshop and a series of writing exercises, plus a tanka book fair and silent auction. You can see the complete schedule on the TSA website. This conference will already be over by the time you read this, but as I write this message, I am greatly looking forward to our latest gathering of the tanka tribes. Because of the pandemic, we hadn't met together since the summer of 2019, so this event feels like another step beyond those challenging times.

Finally, I am also pleased to report on the society's latest elections, with all incumbent officers reelected for the 2023-2024 term. A deep bow of gratitude to all our officers for their work in recent years and for their willingness to continue. In addition, we are very pleased to welcome Ryland Shengzhi Li to the new position of second vice president. We look forward to his fresh ideas for society activities, such as a tanka mentorship program that is already under consideration.

We have much to be thankful for in our organization. The Tanka Society of America would not be what it is today without the influence of Sanford Goldstein. To give him the last word, here's a tanka by Sandy, which won first place in TSA's 2003 International Tanka Contest:

> from my hospital window
> I see across a bare field
> in the morning rain
> a yellow silk umbrella
> on its solitary way

—*Michael Dylan Welch*

Editor's Message

As I prepare to write, I open Sanford Goldstein's new book, *the last mile on the tanka road* (Stark Mountain Press, May 2023). Reading its honest tanka on aging and loneliness, waiting and writing, friendship and tears, I feel him connect with me. I'm just a generation behind him, and things that were in the back of my mind come to the fore. I read the book to the end, marking some tanka I might share. This poignant one, I decide, he has written for us, at this time:

> when we die
> do we leave energy behind
> in the minds of those
> who remember us?
> maybe ghost tanka?

Yes, I think we do. Like him, what poet among us has not wondered and hoped that our tanka live on?

In his President's Message, Michael Dylan Welch has covered upcoming TSA activities for celebrating Sanford's life and his contributions to our tanka world. Ken Slaughter invites tribute poems with his "Tanka Hangout" prompt for the fall issue. And in this issue, we feature Part 1 of "Sanford Goldstein's Tanka World: A Diary of the Emotional Changes in a Man's Life." In it, Randy Brooks lets Goldstein speak for himself, with a generous selection of tanka from his collections and quotations from their introductions and from essays and interviews. It appears in place of our "Poet and Tanka" essay, which is on a brief hiatus but will resume in 2024.

Other sad news. We shall also miss two other notable poets. TSA member Jeannie Lupton, whose candid collection *Love Is a Tanka* was reviewed in our Spring/Summer 2022 issue, passed away March 6. Denis Garrison, who edited and published the journal *Modern English Tanka* and *The Tanka Teachers Guide* (see the TSA website), died February 25. His tanka collaboration with Joy McCall, *Calling Forth the Light*, was reviewed in our last issue. A new, posthumous collection of his work, *At the Gates of Heaven*, is available from Amazon.

Sumi-e. In this issue, our two covers relate in a unique way. Marilyn Fleming's lyrical tanka chosen for the back cover touches on *sumi-e*, the Japanese monochromatic ink painting originally developed in China during the Sung dynasty (960-1274); Zen Buddhist monks took it to Japan in the mid-1300s. (See "The Back Cover" for more on her poem.) The technique still inspires painters—among them, our front cover artist for 2023, Emma Alexander Arthur. This issue's cover especially suggests sumi-e, with Arthur's bold black-ink strokes, creative use of empty space and, of course, the Enso.

Of her inspiration, she says that years ago during a struggle with chronic illness she discovered the "healing and transformative effects" of Zen arts "such as sumi-e, tai chi qigong shibashi, meditation and haiku writing . . . . Sumi-e captivated me with its meditative nature. I started by painting the Enso, created with a single breath and brushstroke, that encapsulates the essence of Zen philosophy."

Submission guidelines updated. First, about the "Selected Tanka" and "Sequences and Strings"/"Responsive Tanka" sections, which I edit: I love receiving and reviewing our contributors' work and have tried to allow poets some choice in submissions. Currently, poets are welcome to submit up to ten unpublished, original tanka *or* two tanka sequences/strings (not more than six tanka in each) *or* one tanka sequence/string and up to five individual tanka. What we haven't spelled out before (and may cause confusion) is this: From among these, one individual tanka *or* a sequence/string may be selected for the issue. Not both.

An added tip for poets sending individual tanka to me: Even though I select just one tanka, I suggest submitting the full ten or five tanka allowed. That gives me some choice as editor and gives you a better chance of acceptance.

We also publish essays and interviews, and these submissions come to me as well. However, as space in the journal for these is limited, I encourage you to email me in advance with a summary of what you intend—especially if you are writing the piece specifically with us in mind. (Our "Poet and Tanka" essays are by invitation.)

—*Susan Weaver*

Tanka Hangout

In Tanka Hangout we're pleased to continue the Member's Choice Award. The winning poet receives a $25 honorarium and selects a new winner from among the poems appearing in this section, awards up to three honorable mentions, and comments on these choices in an essay for the next issue—thus continuing the cycle.

Member's Choice Tanka
Elinor Pihl Huggett

What an honor it was to have my tanka selected as Member's Choice Tanka! Now I have the pleasure and honor of choosing my own favorites. I almost hesitate to say "favorites" because they are all good, but I selected a few that personally resonate with me. What a wonderful group of gifted artists we have that contribute to *Ribbons*.

Here is my Member's Choice Award:

> childhood evenings . . .
> those mellow notes from
> Grandfather's violin
> made cares of the day
> drift into moonlight

Catherine Smith, Sydney, Australia

This gentle, peaceful tanka brings back memories of a time when the pace was slower, when we relied on walking, streetcars, and maybe even horse and wagon. It reminds me of the many times spent at my grandma and grandpa's house in Chicago and later when they lived with us. I get a concrete image of home, with the extended family bringing us comfort of the familiar, stability, and wisdom of our elders.

What were the cares of the day? For Mom, she could put her apron aside now that meals and housekeeping were done and the kids were home. For the kids, they could close the book on school and homework. For Dad, his workday was over and he could relax.

Soon it would be bedtime stories and lights out.

1st Honorable Mention:

> not the loud
> not the herculean
> but a warbling wren
> singing
> from the cedar

Elizabeth Black, Haymarket, VA

Perhaps with all the clamor of the day we have to endure, we've learned to block out traffic noise, action films, TV babble and the uproar of sports games. What sounds really speak to our souls? I would like to think it's the purring of a kitten, the chatter of a toddler, and the warble of a wren "singing/ from the cedar."

2nd Honorable Mention:

> teenage freedom
> was a car of my own
> with a radio
> tuned in to the music
> forbidden by my parents

Keitha Keyes, Sydney, Australia

Here is a tanka that is pure fun. Who hasn't, after years under the watchful eyes of teachers and dependence on parents, wanted to kick up their heels and do their own thing for a change? Is the writer feeling a tad naughty, with no fear being caught, being grounded, or being sent to the principal's office?

* * *

Tanka Hangout: Compassion

> her row veering off
> the peasant woman plants
> toward her crying child
> —Issa (1763-1828)

Welcome to the second edition of the Tanka Hangout! For the prompt I chose a haiku by Issa because I wanted to receive poems that speak of empathy and compassion. I was particularly interested in compassion for strangers, fellow travelers on this planet whom we've never met. I received a variety of interesting poems, which explore the topic from a range of perspectives.

Issa was known for his poems about insects and other small creatures, and there are several of those represented here. Genie Nakano writes about crawling on her hands and knees to blow a spider out the door. Madhuri Pillai recounts burying a magpie that was hit by a car. Ryland Li shows us the sheer beauty of a spider web: "Humans," he says, "build with the labor of our bodies; spiders build not only with the labor of their bodies, but with their bodies in and of themselves." He compares their webs to a human creation: "a compact disc" glittering "in the sun."

On a lighter note, I was amused by Tim Cremin's poem, in which the narrator opens a window to let a fly out, and two more fly in. I could certainly relate to that one. I could also relate to Marilyn Fleming's poem, in which she complains about those "damn crickets" chirping till dawn.

Some poets included skillful references to Issa in their poems. Mari Konno writes: "I live in an aging town with deep snow in winter. In spring lots of pretty dandelions bloom, swaying merrily in the breeze. The scene reminds me of Issa's village filled with children as snow melts." Neal Whitman is "perplexed by Bashō's indifference to the child on the road" in his well-known work, *Road to the Interior*. Neal imagines an admonition from Issa to Bashō: "pick up that orphan baby."

I received many touching portraits of family members. Stacie Dye writes passionately "about my sister and her recent diagnosis with dementia." Joy McCall recalls her daughter's love for a horse: "Cloud was the horse my Wendy used to ride, before the MS made her ride a wheelchair like me." Ruth Holzer submitted a heartfelt poem about caring for a mother who no longer recognizes her. David Hill writes about his father, who worked long hours at two jobs: "He became a stranger to his own family and I think he regretted it. Later," David says, "I realized that I had become just like my father, hence the echo of my dad." Speaking of fathers, James Haddad writes about his father: "Sometimes it takes an alarming situation to bring out the best in someone. In my early years, WWII beckoned to me and Dad drove me to Camp Pendleton. I could feel his pride, but his love, never before openly expressed, [really] came through."

And there are many empathetic depictions of strangers. Adelaide B. Shaw gives us a touching portrait of a woman tending to her handicapped child. Chen-ou Liu shows us a scene at a hospital, with an injured (abused?) mother and a child cowering in a corner of the waiting room. We also meet homeless people and a woman missing two front teeth. Jim Chessing comments about his poem: "Even a homeless person can have a work ethic, in this case picking recyclables out of public cans."

And then there is Fishbones. According to Sigrid Saradunn, "Fishbones, a Depression hobo, always had his mouth organ with him. His teen nephew brought his guitar. After a relative died, the family gathered around the room to honor brother and granddad. The oldest and younger would start playing without speaking."

Something we don't always speak about: not all our attempts at being compassionate go well. Do our good intentions even matter, or are they all that matter, as Jerome Berglund asks in his poem about, of all things, removing an appendix. Robert Erlandson tells about attempting to reach out to a man, apparently drunk, who is lying on the ground. Robert is not so cordially invited to "piss off." Here is his comment: "This happened—however, I have not used the same language he did. I doubt the language is suitable for the journal."

A few of these poems challenge us to be better. At times, human beings are kinder to insects than they are to their own family members, as Sally Biggar points out. Anete Chaney describes a boy wearing a dress, and the unkind whispers that follow. Gerry Jacobson writes about visiting an Indian guru known as "The Mother" and urges us to "find a Way." Susan Burch sounds a note of hope that we might come to accept the aliens among us. I hope these poems help, in some way, to bring out the better angels in all of us. That's one reason why I chose the theme. Enjoy the poems!

—*Ken Slaughter*

first light
first thought is of her mother
then the day's routine
floods in with brazen sunlight
she cannot work her grief away

Margi Abraham, Sydney, Australia

row after row
of flowery perfection—
she gently places
the sad, rejected plants
in her shopping cart

Mary Frederick Ahearn, South Coventry, PA

autism
awareness day—
my son
begins to notice
birdsong

Jenny Ward Angyal, Gibsonville, NC

today I cope
with others' sorrows
beyond my own . . .
the total eclipse
of a global heart

an'ya, Florence, OR

neighbourhood party
islands of friends
I reach out
to the solitary
wallflower

   Joanna Ashwell, Barnard Castle, UK

        good intentions:
        meaningless
        or most important part—
        examining
        an appendix

           Jerome Berglund, Minneapolis, MN

I was vulnerable—
never as protected
as the spiders
you always coaxed
out of harm's way

   Sally Biggar, Topsham, ME

        feathers, petals
        gumnuts and pebbles
        washday treasures
        in my child's pocket
        that nature bequeaths

          Michelle Brock, Queanbeyan, Australia

silver bells
she tells me a story
I should have
known
years ago

   Randy Brooks, Taylorville, IL

nameless bag lady
who fed the pigeons
I carve a bird
in the fading green paint
of her empty park bench

   John Budan, Newberg, OR

        a barge
        floating down the river
        slowly
        we come to accept
        the aliens among us

           Susan Burch, Hagerstown, MD

the wood thrush
sings the sun up
arm in arm
I sit with you to share
this biting grief

   Pris Campbell, Lake Worth, FL

        the old man
        blows blood from his nose
        is this the day
        he performs
        seventy pushups

           David Chandler, Chicago, IL

the pirouette
of a princess dress
with a little boy inside
now the whispers
who are dresses for

   Anette Chaney, Harrison, AR

expression the same
no matter the outcome
this modern man
going from can to can
the tide washes over him

   Jim Chessing, San Ramon, CA

        patio dining
        a sparrow lands
        on my table
        eyeing my sandwich
        with envy

           Jackie Chou, Pico Rivera, CA

once again
the junco builds her nest
in my hanging fuchsia
when I see the pale blue eggs
I stop watering

   Margaret Chula, Portland, OR

        after the harvest
        the corners of the field
        feed the poor, the children,
        however wanting
        they are welcome here

           Linda Conroy, Bellingham, WA

in the hedges
i planted with my neighbor
to keep our lives separate
two birds chatter
like old friends

   Christopher Costabile, Valrico, FL

spring morning
in the studio
I lift the sash
to let a fly out
two others fly in

   Tim Cremin, Andover, MA

        a young boy
        picks fruit all day long,
        all summer long . . .
        sixty years later
        he still won't eat a strawberry

          Mary Davila, Buffalo, NY

summer pond
flame skimmer
guards his mate
as she lays her eggs
dotbydotbydotbydot

   Marcyn Del Clements, Claremont, CA

        every mom and dad
        frets over their babies
        baby ducklings
        swim all in a row
        behind their mama

          Jack Douthitt, Fox Point, WI

this specter
crept into our lives
intent on taking you—
hold on to my hand,
I won't let you slip away

   stacey dye, Thomasville, GA

lying by the curb
I rushed to his aid
kneeling
touching his shoulder, he spat—
"Piss off, go away, I'm drunk"

   Robert Erlandson, Birmingham, MI

        called from the trance
        of my workday walk
        I retrace my steps . . .
        the customary "hello"
        from the kind-eyed beech

          Claire Everett, Northallerton, England

she wakes
in that silence after snow
the air
above the bassinet
and her baby . . . quite still

   Amelia Fielden, Wollongong, Australia

        she looked like a toy
        in the bottom of the pail
        perhaps from last fall
        just another field mouse
        no longer cold or hungry

          Michael Flanagan, Woodbury, MN

summer heat
the damn cricket
chirp
chirp chirping
until cockcrow

   Marilyn Fleming, Pewaukee, WI

bodysurfing
a wave crests
and curls
the dolphin and I
both smiling

   William Scott Galasso, Laguna Woods, CA

        the wonderful
        drive together on the way
        to WW II
        wishing the best for me, he said,
        El Paso next, another world

          James Haddad, Pasadena, CA

spring winds carry
a man's accordion tunes . . .
with him a young boy
holding a sign that asks
for spare change

   Johnnie Johnson Hafernik, San Francisco, CA

        tuning
        his ancient shamisen
        with gentle touch
        he sings songs of love
        to his unborn son

          Hazel Hall, Aranda, Australia

a mix
of dark clouds and sun
stopping by
with two cups of coffee
on your retirement day

   Jon Hare, Falmouth, MA

dew be do be dew
Sinatra sings Issa
strangers in the night
I think of those I have helped
and of those who've helped me

   Charles Harmon, Whittier, CA

                I scoop our grandchild
                above that rogue wave
                my toes cling
                to dissolving sand
                stronger than Neptune

                    Carole Harrison, Jamberoo, Australia

the slim crust
of a new moon rising
I share
what's left of my supper
with nobody's dog

   Michele L. Harvey, Hamilton, NY

                my father's footsteps
                fading as he walks away
                echos of the man
                in search of recognition
                turn my path away from you

                    David Lee Hill, Bakersfield, CA

I carefully bathe
the worn body that bore me
a lifetime ago
she asks me again
where is my daughter

   Ruth Holzer, Herndon, VA

my son
still in grade school
gifts
his gold coin allowance
to a homeless man

   Marilyn Humbert, Berowra Heights, Australia

        multitasking—
        a new mother
        works remotely
        on her laptop
        a colicky baby

           Rick Jackofsky, Rocky Point, NY

on our knees
we crawl to receive
her blessing . . .
this world
must find a Way

   Gerry Jacobson, Canberra, Australia

        sound asleep
        in her comfy carrier
        the sightless tabby
        will soon board an airliner
        to cross an ocean to us

           Roberta Beach Jacobson, Indianola, IA

shuffling with shame
he asked just for a dollar
I hurried on by
unable to gaze
'til his shame became mine

   William Kerr, New York, NY

she stood in the twilight
looking down the road
till long after
his taillights
had disappeared

   Michael Ketchek, Rochester, NY

        at the vet's
        a couple with an old dog
        caressing him
        crying their goodbyes
        . . . then the door is closed

           Keitha Keyes, Sydney, Australia

giant toad inside
the comfort station
i prop the door
tadpoles swarm the lake's edge
in the valley below

   Roy Kindelberger, Edmonds, WA

        fortitude
        against the power,
        the skinny frog
        must be you, Issa . . .
        rooting for you

           Mariko Kitakubo, Tokyo, Japan

could it be said
any clearer . . .
the cat
asleep on my shoulder
paw resting on my cheek

   Kathy Kituai, Canberra, Australia

dandelions
instead of children
fill
my village now
as snow melts

   Mari Konno, Fukui, Japan

        haunting violin
        plays softly in the background
        holding back
        my tears for your dad
        I give you a hug

          Don LaMure, Fremont, CA

I held doors
for women and gave them
the sidewalk . . .
now, sometimes, they
do the same for the old guy

   Peter Larsen, Lake View Terrace, CA

        an owl hoots
        as a late winter snow
        shrouds the pines—
        footprints fade away
        down the snowy path

          Michael H. Lester, Los Angeles, CA

compact disc
rippling in the sun
thread
by thread
out of his tiny body

   Ryland Shengzhi Li, Arlington, VA

red gathering
in a mother's puffy eyes . . .
her boy alone
in the shadowed corner
of the hospital hallway

   Chen-ou Liu, Ajax, Canada

       black phoebes play
       around the edge of my dream
       singing the high notes . . .
       may mourning doves greet us
       on the other side

          Janis Albright Lukstein, Rancho Palos Verdes, CA

the crushed bee's nest
and her son's welted legs
with each tweezer pull
his tears, her kisses
and a prayer

   Richard L. Matta, San Diego, CA

       she named
       the dappled horse Cloud
       for its mane was grey
       like the dark sky
       on a stormy day

          Joy McCall, Norwich, England

she cash apps
her thirty-year-old daughter
gas money —
raindrops tap
this rented car's windshield

   Lenard D. Moore, Raleigh, NC

on my
hands and knees
I blow
a baby spider
out the door

   Genie Nakano, Gardena, CA

      receding flood
      whining of the mother cat
      through the howling wind
      even soft wooded trees
      showing resilience

         Suraj Nanu, Kerala, India

a mom worried
about her child's breathing—
in bright light
lips and fingers blue
a fast trip to the ER

   David F. Noble, Charlottesville, VA

      three ants
      drag a moth
      across the patio
      co-operation
      among the smallest

         James B. Peters, Cottontown, TN

a wildflower posie
left on my doorstep
how unexpected
this kindness, and yet
it too is true

   Dru Philippou, Taos, NM

another car
stills the still fluttering
feathers . . .
i bury the magpie
under a flowering camellia

   Madhuri Pillai, Melbourne, Australia

              sunshine at last
              dappling the leaves
              bent in the storm:
              I catch his voice cruising on
              about cars, boats & motorbikes

                 Patricia Prime, New Zealand

we are
each of us waves
forming
to rise up for a time
only to disappear

   Carol Raisfeld, Atlantic Beach, NY

              just when I thought
              she was out of love
              my wife
              starts giving food
              to all the strays

                 Bryan Rickert, Belleville, IL

his running
along the river path
more of a hobble . . .
his twisted foot
& the long wait for surgery

   Elaine Riddell, Hamilton, New Zealand

missing two front teeth
her dress a faded red
she thanks me
for the food pantry box
hugs her young daughter

Ed Rielly, Westbrook, ME

    sleeve dangling, a sloughed
    snakeskin (or cocoon?): he's lost
    an arm to sepsis . . .
    as I grope for some resistance
    a void knocks me off balance

    Michael Sandler, Mercer Island, WA

home from the gravesite
Fishbones and his grand-nephew
play the blues
as the family gathers
'round—no words needed

Sigrid Saradunn, Bar Harbor, ME

    tender love—
    mated sparrows feeding seed
    beak-to-beak . . .
    couple in the nest
    share their seed with young

    Don Sharp, Jr, Sagle, ID

handicapped child
again and again his mother
wipes away the drool;
her patient smile,
the gift of angels

Adelaide B. Shaw, Somers, NY

the old man tells me
when he was three
his mother left
day after day he watched
the red bus come . . . and go

   Catherine Smith, Sydney, Australia

               she listens
               to his weeping—
               the bee flew away
               so quickly,
               in the playground

                  Jane Stuart, Flatwoods, KY

in the playground
a broken robin's egg
her little hand
folds more deeply
into mine

   Margaret Tau, New Bern, NC

               stopped in mid-sentence
               my eyes follow you
               across the room
               my heart's been here for years
               just didn't know it

                  Mark Teaford, Napa, CA

spring sun—
her light in cumuli
still on the mountain
a man chants Buddha's name
among eternal snow

   Xenia Tran, Nairn, Scotland

homeless
in a shop doorway
the old man's humiliation
after such a long
and largely honourable life

   Susan Mary Wade, Littlehampton, England

        near the creek's edge
        a thrashing fish on the line
        I call for help—
        not to land it
        but to quickly let it go!

           Patricia Wakimoto, Gardena, CA

flow reduced
we share the shower
a spider and I
until hair wash day . . .
I move it to the sink

   Joanne Watcyn-Jones, Sydney, Australia

        Georgia traffic stop—
        dogs sniff the girls' underwear
        for drugs
        a lacrosse team humiliated
        for traveling while Black

           Susan Weaver, Allentown, PA

human beings
seem always to be doing
—takers or givers—
a nudge for us from Issa
pick up that orphan baby

   Neal Whitman, Pacific Grove, CA

at the beach
with our little shovels
sandcastle dreams
the breakwater my mother makes
with her heart while we sleep

   Kath Abela Wilson, Pasadena, CA

          a thorny path
          for a ten-year-old
          between two homes
          despite our tenuous link
          she gives me little hugs

               Beatrice Yell, Sydney, Australia

Next Theme: Tribute Poems

As you know, the leading pioneer of English-language tanka, Sanford Goldstein, passed away on May 5 at 97. Dr. Goldstein, or Sandy (as he was called by most who knew him) was influential as both a tanka poet and as a translator of modernist Japanese poets. For our next Tanka Hangout theme, we invite members to submit tribute poems honoring this towering master of the tanka form. (For more on Sanford Goldstein, see Part 1 of "Sanford Goldstein's Tanka World" by Randy Brooks in this issue.)

    If, instead, you would like to write a tribute to someone who was a seminal influence in your personal life, feel free to do so. Tanka Hangout will be presented in two sections. The first will be tributes to Sanford Goldstein. The next will contain all the other tribute poems.

    Send your submission to tsahangout@outlook.com in the body of an email, with "Tanka Hangout" as the subject heading. Please, no attachments, and please—send one and only one poem! Email is the preferred method, but you can also mail your submission to:

Ken Slaughter
Tanka Hangout Editor
24 Briarwood Circle
Worcester, MA 01606

Beneath the poem, include your full name as you wish it to appear, with your town or city of residence and its location (state/province and country). The deadline is August 31, 2023. For further guidelines, see the last page of the journal.

—*Ken Slaughter*

from park trees
the chortles and chirps
of courting
deep-seated in my soul
sweet sounding swallow song

an'ya

Selected Tanka

dreams in one hand
daydreams in the other
light split
equally on this chilly
spring equinox

   Pris Campbell, Lake Worth, FL

                in April
                a small black snake
                lies in glittering sunlight
                on the white bridge
                to the shrine

                    Aya Yuhki, Tokyo, Japan

fairy wren darting
here . . . there . . . everywhere
this spring
how could one lifetime
ever be enough?

   Michelle Brock, Queanbeyan, Australia

                new buds
                on my magnolia
                just days old
                when did I last read Faulkner
                or dream of red clay roads?

                    Michael L. Evans, Puyallup, WA

magnolia
in full purple bloom
what other love notes
have I missed
in my hibernation?

   Julie Thorndyke, Sydney, Australia

        some days
        after the storm
        the umbrella still
        open, covered
        with pink petals

        Ryland Shengzhi Li, Arlington, VA

the seeds
I wish to plant
I preserve
fragrance of memories
under the drizzling rain

   Pravat Kumar Padhy, Bhubaneswar, India

        ripples travel
        through spring's tall grass
        on a grey wooden bench
        you lift your head
        from my shoulder

        Ian Gwin, Seattle, WA

a boy's red kite
lifts above the beach
we watch
it waving in the wind
his joy of holding onto air

   Margi Abraham, Sydney, Australia

circus spotlight
spins on her neck loop cord
high above the crowd
no net below
holding my breath until she's safe

   Sharon Lynne Yee, Torrance, CA

        summer fog
        Bach's coffee cantata fills
        the kitchen
        trees appear . . . disappear
        the soprano line

           Johnnie Johnson Hafernik, San Francisco, CA

the magpie
taking flight as
i approach
leaving her song hanging
on the clothesline

   Madhuri Pillai, Melbourne, Australia

        moon rays
        inside the unfolding
        banana blossom . . .
        I open my window
        to a new summer dawn

           Lakshmi Iyer, Kerala, India

a hummingbird
sampling the garden
hesitates
examining me
and seeing no blooms

   John S. Gilbertson, Greenville, SC

willow branches caress
their watery reflections . . .
along the shore
a swarm of dragonflies
helicopter into view

  Jack Douthitt, Fox Point, WI

        night falls
        small lights dance
        in front of us
        we suddenly remember
        the safest journey home

          Xenia Tran, Nairn, Scotland

after the squall
hundreds of fallen plums . . .
i offer
their bottled sweetness
to my friends

  Rupa Anand, New Delhi, India

        tiny insects flash
        through a shaft
        of sunlight—
        a meteor shower
        in my backyard

          David F. Noble, Charlottesville, VA

a slow stream
in a rock-quiet place
stealing these hours
is not a sin
wasting them is

  Tim Cremin, Andover, MA

crickets chirp
deep into evening
I remember
the honeysuckle taste
of summer romance

   Theresa A. Cancro, Wilmington, DE

        at last
        my childhood-self
        blossoms
        a soft side of innocence
        the prickly side of reality

           Carol Raisfeld, Atlantic Beach, NY

clandestine
documents
unearthed everywhere—
finding my diary
mom has questions

   Bonnie J Scherer, Palmer, AK

        razed movie house
        moldy popcorn
        in dusty carpets
        we never made it
        beyond first base

           John Budan, Newberg, OR

my leg brushes
against the white ghost
of a dandelion—
in my heedless youth
how many seeds did I sow?

   Curt Pawlisch, Madison, WI

neighborhood park
the empty basketball court
i used to play on—
from netless hoops a whisper
of forgotten swishes

   Roy Kindelberger, Edmonds, WA

        sprinkled
        on the mountain
        sugar-cube villas
        lit by tapas bars . . .
        we accelerate up the hill

          Joanne Watcyn-Jones, Sydney, Australia

matching faces
with our senior yearbook,
so many strangers . . .
I fumble for bonbons
in a bowl of walnuts

   Peter Larsen, Lake View Terrace, CA

        wind swirls
        watching the kite dance
        feeling you
        skywrite from heaven
        how much you miss me

          Don LaMure, Fremont, CA

the empty spaces
between people—
leaving room for those we love
and miss
in the photo

   Sophia Conway, Nanoose Bay, Canada

twenty years
since opening this suitcase
memory trip
I feel your touch again
tingle with our first kiss

   Robert Erlandson, Birmingham, MI

        top of the tree
        an aerie of twigs
        my heart keeps
        a nest of old loves
            not forgotten

        Ricardo J. Bogaert-Alvarez, Denver, CO

awakening
the evolving chatbot asks
if i know love
her invisible selfies
sparkle with hope

   Ramund Ro, Hong Kong, China

        fog clears
        above the tree canopy
        I search
        constellations
        for signs of you

        C.X. Turner, Birmingham, UK

gray beach stone
carried in his pocket
on my desk
silence of the ocean surf
echoing in my pen

   Teri White Carns, Anchorage, AK

a wren's song
waves crashing
poetry
the smell of rain—
I am all these things

   stacey dye, Thomasville, GA

        finches
        have deserted
        the jacaranda . . .
        sitting at the desk to write
        my words spill over themselves

           Patricia Prime, Auckland, New Zealand

snow geese
spreading to chaos
across the sky
within me, a voice
is ready to be different

   Richa Sharma, Ghaziabad, India

        six-mile hike
        up the switchbacks
        breathing in
        writing out
        the hour's tanka

           David Chandler, Chicago, IL

flowers in wet grass
a graceful wind
nudging plates and tablecloth
conversation fluttering
words for my newest song

   Linda Conroy, Bellingham, WA

stuck in the middle—
a sparrow
sitting by my window
chirps
the rest of the poem

   Ram Chandran, Madurai, India

               the salt
               of buttered popcorn
               lingers
               after writing
               into early night

               Lenard D. Moore, Raleigh, NC

I'm writing
under the blue moonlight
in the town
where in ancient times
Yakamochi edited *Man'yoshu*

   Mari Konno, Fukui, Japan

               my eyes closed
               through one-third of my life . . .
               imagine
               all the tanka I could write
               if I didn't need sleep

               Mary Davila, Buffalo, NY

to give meaning
is said to be the last
stage of grief
will my tanka in the end
become birdsong

   Kath Abela Wilson, Pasadena, CA

with the turn of a page
I'm in Tudor England
stirring pottage
in a smoky kitchen—
armchair travel

   Kathryn J. Stevens, Cary, NC

       forgoing
       my usual book
       I snuggle in
       remembering
       childhood bedtimes

          Bob Loomis, Concord, CA

my son asks me
about the meaning of life
I put a finger to my lips
then point to our kittens
asleep in the sun

   Joshua St. Claire, York County, PA

       an owl's wing
       spans the Milky Way
       that instant
       your news changed
       the colour of my forever

          Carole Harrison, Jamberoo, Australia

I drive down the road
your words hovering
a wind lifting
my thoughts—
cottonwood seeds

   Janet Ruth Heller, Portage, MI

forgotten
the name of that slope . . .
shadow tag
with my mother
when her smile was young

   Mariko Kitakubo, Tokyo, Japan

        sudden glow in the field
        after the passing rain
        dandelion blossoms
        the little boy picks
        for his mother as she weeds

        Wai Mei Wong, Toronto, Canada

the lipstick
mother wore, fire engine red
a warning
for all to stand back
and not follow too closely

   Michele L. Harvey, Hamilton, NY

        these old
        training wheels
        how I still
        find it hard
        to let you go

        Bryan Rickert, Belleville, IL

the blue veins
on the back of my hands
a map from my father
shows me
the way home

   Robert Stone, Coram, NY

in the empty hours
searching the pages
of his war diary
for his face
before I was born

   kathryn liebowitz, Groton, MA

        clearing mom's house . . .
        dad's old bridge coat
        from the war
        found in the garage
        a nesting place for rats

           Charles Harmon, Los Angeles, CA

Dad's birthday
a true Gemini
he's both
here and not here
at the same time

   Ruth Holzer, Herndon, VA

        a paper cigar ring
        tucked deep inside sofa cushions
        for years
        memories of my father
        rise up and curl around me

           Barbara Kaufmann, Massapequa Park, NY

his wife would complain
always ocha — never water
yet in loving remembrance
of his long-lived life
scoops of green tea ice cream

   Patricia Wakimoto, Gardena, CA

a rose
in an ice cream cone—
his love
was never quite
as I epected

    Barbara Curnow, Canberra, Australia

        sichuan dumplings
        in a slippery chili sauce
        enjoying
        the repartee
        of our chopsticks

            Jon Hare, Falmouth, MA

white space
between plum blossoms
sumi-e
the way we are close
but not too close

    Marilyn Fleming, Pewaukee, WI

        the red-tailed hawk
        spreads her wings and lets
        the warm air hold her . . .
        never have I felt so myself
        as this moment with you

            Jim Chessing, San Ramon, CA

busy worker bees
kissing blossoms
in my lover's secret garden
sweet retreat
from prying eyes

    David Lee Hill, Bakersfield, CA

dreaming of my wife
when young
covered only in moonlight
    it wakes me up
     . . . wishing

Don M. Sharp, Jr., Sagle, ID

        the quiet
        after a storm—
        I lie waiting
        for your kiss after
        the lovemaking

Mona Bedi, Delhi, India

integral equation =
trying 2
figure out (x)
if you care [about me]
at all

Susan Burch, Hagerstown, MD

        "please don't judge me
        too harshly," she yawned,
        "we're just different people"—
        the words I have picked over
        for four seasons now

C.W. Blackburn, Dorset, United Kingdom

mornings—
summer fog
caresses the hill
like a lover who kisses
then disappears

Gail Brooks, Laguna Beach, CA

sunrise, coffee
a Kerouac impulse
to chuck the clock
ramble under spacious skies
free, rapt, beholden to one

   William Scott Galasso, Laguna Woods, CA

        evening heat
        a faraway plane catches
        the sun's last rays
        at this age still wanting
        unattainable things

           Jan O'Loughlin, Sydney, Australia

our trio of cups,
charged with light and
pledged to this unending moment's joy
we know cannot last . . .
and so we dance

   Kathleen Beavers, Las Vegas, NV

        the tram
        crammed with travellers
        a crowd of stories
        in progress
        —mine near the end

           Simon Wilson, Nottingham, UK

imagination—
walking the streets
of New Orleans
I breathe the bourbon
of my younger years

   Jane Stuart, Flatwoods, KY

eavesdropping—
three older women
talk of aging
I hear the boring echo
       of myself

Adelaide B. Shaw, Somers, NY

        a birthday party
        for a ninety-three-year-old
        one card says
        consider your childhood over
        what a pity that would be

Peter Barker, Manchester, England

haircut day
I need something new
surprise me
with a pastel color
and a shorter bob

Roberta Beach Jacobson, Indianola, IA

        my years
        are my riches
        just a few left
        but oh
        the run I've had

Jeannie Lupton, Berkeley, CA

floating
through a portal
of a new unknown
in the silence
I dream myself young

Barbara Sayre, Winchester, TN

just a low rumble
of the vending machine
in a waiting room
my heart cries out loud
to know the truth

   Christine L. Villa, North Highlands, CA

        it's so hard
        to see her slipping away
        purple irises
        hold the memories
        she has lost

           Heather Lurie, Rangiora, New Zealand

beside camellia trimmings
strewn on grass
an empty chair—
his illness hides
in the shadows

   Anne Curran, Hamilton, New Zealand

        visiting father
        at rest in the hospice ...
        all day rain
        the sound of my
        breaking heart

           C. William Hinderliter, Phoenix, AZ

deep in terrible heat
autumn begins
grieving
louder and louder cicadas sing
death's distant harmony

   Robert Witmer, Tokyo, Japan

a wilderness grows
around me as I wait
I ache
to visit face to face
beyond this habitation

   Jeanne Cook, South Bend, IN

        hardly a stirring
        in the windless pines . . .
        the sun sets
        and rises
        on my grief

           Michael Dylan Welch, Sammamish, WA

lake fishing . . .
remembering him
as I cinch a blood knot
tendrils of dusk
sink into darkness

   Richard L. Matta, San Diego, CA

        clearing out
        his apartment
        after twenty years
        the boxes she sent
        left unopened

           Debbie Olson, Syracuse, NY

his old family home
nothing left except
creaking floorboards
and an unsettling medley
of long ago voices

   Catherine Smith, Sydney, Australia

after dark
the buzz of a bee
gathering nectar
so many things I wish
I'd made time to say

   Kathy Kituai, Canberra, Australia

        the full moon
        shrouded by dark clouds
        a breakthrough
        I reveal my yin side
        learning to say no

           Jackie Chou, Pico Rivera, CA

learning frog pose
a squat handstand—
    all the rockiness
    till i inhabit
the point of balance

   Mira Walker, Yarralumla, Australia

        away from
        my safe place—
        jackdaw
        nesting
        in a chimney pot

           Alan Peat, Biddulph, UK

fingerlings
break the lake's surface
in eights and tens
with threats from beneath
bedsheets twisted at dawn

   Rodney Williams, Trafalgar, Australia

after rain
grey slugs with red warnings
and carnivorous leopards*
stuff of childhood
nightmares

   Margaret Conley, Hunters Hill, Australia

       daffodils pushing
       upward through mud
       & snow flurries
       like my life
       this mid-March morning

          Marilyn Shoemaker Hazelton, Allentown, PA

night within us
and the sky without
a single star
to lead us
to each other

   Maxianne Berger, Outremont, Canada

       everyone I knew
       came home broken
       in some way
       from that endless
       forever war

          Jeffrey Walthall, Fairfax, VA

rain taps
the post office windows
the man on the MISSING poster
was once a boy who slept
in my blanket fort

   Joshua Michael Stewart, Ware, MA

*This, the longer of the two slugs, grows to 20 centimeters (almost 8 inches).

lost sycamores
no longer shade the children
playing on a city street . . .
gone, too, are the things with wings
that launched their dreams of flight

   Dru Philippou, Taos, NM

        searching
        for keys to unlock
        my mind
        what I see all around
        are walls and more walls

           Kala Ramesh, Pune, India

prison visit over
she stops at mcdonald's
eats his sins
past, present
and those he's yet to do

   Steve Black, Reading, UK

        the apple orchard
        where I stole for lunch
        just another street now
        of identical houses
        and identical smiles

           Nicholas Klacsanzky, Burien, WA

birds of a feather
under the banyan tree
a child dreams
of a tomorrow
without suspicion

   Srini, Madanapalle, India

homecoming
the abandoned cat with kittens
an unwed mother
takes her bath
in the lonely ghat

   Suraj Nanu, Kerala, India

        every day
        in the pasture
        cows and calves . . .
        old white male politicians
        in women's lives

          James B. Peters, Cottontown, TN

the boy's collie
missing for days . . .
a neighbor saying
it was chasing his sheep
before he shot it

   Edward J. Rielly, Westbrook, ME

        weeping willow . . .
        where you last lay down
        paws folded
        autumn earth still warm
        my shovel heavy

          Betsy Hearne, Urbana, IL

Athena's tags
I mosaicked to the headstone
her collar
never returned by the vet
unless it's in the ashes

   Diane Funston, Marysville, CA

deep dusk
at the road
even a fox
looks both ways
before crossing

   Anthony Lusardi, Rockaway Borough, NJ

        amazingly good aim
        for a two-week-old filly . . .
        the old scar
        of a small hoof print
        on my husband's chin

          Elinor Pihl Huggett, Lakeville, IN

strangely, I'd cooked
meals for a month
filled the freezer
as though in readiness
for my broken arm

   Margaret Owen Ruckert, Sydney, Australia

        my hopeful self
        plants veggies in dry spring
        and nurtures them—
        just as they ripen they are cheap
        in the grocery bins

          Christa Pandey, Austin, TX

down
among the chair legs
looking
for the final piece
of the jigsaw

   Mark Gilbert, Nottingham, UK

a snake's molt quivers
on the crumbling sidewalk
am I
too comfortable
in my skin?

   Kathleen Caster Mace, Niwot, CO

        the Northern sky
        dancing ribbons of light
        remind me
        not all is predictable
        not all should be known

           David Greenwood, Basking Ridge, NJ

a few steps onto
the Appalachian Trail
and it takes us
far out of ourselves
—the stillness in tall trees

   Robert Kusch, Piscataway, NJ

        a forest stream
        splashes down rock slides
        around boulders
        from one pool to the next . . .
        an ancient song

           Elaine Riddell, Hamilton, New Zealand

a family
of migrants
building a nest
under the freeway—
cliff swallows

   Rick Jackofsky, Rocky Point, NY

on my walk
jay squawk, a fox
and that lingering skunk scent
I take my place
in the universe

   Lesley Anne Swanson, Coopersburg, PA

              eyes and legs twitch
              suspended
              on a silk line
              the spiderling
              dreams on . . . *

            Linda Weir, Ellicott City, MD

fluttering through
the red light
a migrating
painted lady
I touch the brakes

   Marcyn Del Clements, Claremont, CA

              the river
              is dedicated
              to swan, heron & kingfisher
              dawn will always come
              with wings

            AA Marcoff, Leatherhead, England

this water
in this river
will never be here again
jumping in
to see where it goes

   Mark Teaford, Napa, CA

*A new study found jumping spiders may have REM sleep and thus may dream.

taking flight
the wild duck leaves
a trail of droplets . . .
this sudden yen
for a skipping stone

   Sally Biggar, Topsham, ME

        wind sways leaves
        branches bow
        I too
        am wind, shadows,
        leaves, bowing trees

          Carole Glasser Langille, Black Point, Canada

the garden Buddha
and I
dusted with pollen
in stillness
we smile

   Margaret Tau, New Bern, NC

        starry night
        feels like velvet
        to my eyes
            I fall up
        into endless inky sky

          Jennifer Gurney, Broomfield, CO

in the dark
nest of half-dream
I await the birds
who call the new day
up from the sea

   Jen Meader, Richmond, ME

high flying gulls
and the tang of salt air
at Gosman's dock
we always thought
we would sail forever

bkaufmann

Tanka Sequences and Strings

An Aussie Blessing
Hazel Hall, Aranda, Australia

I wish you
an Aussie bluebell sky
a sun-smile
sonic booms of cockatoos
a kookaburra's laugh

washed
from the throat of a shell
one perfect pearl
showers of white lilacs
on a moonbeam's path

seventy
different wildflowers
with mingled scents
a gum tree garlanded
with countless stars

an apricot tree
for climbing through
your dreams
a country kitchen
with blackened hearth

At Giverny
Mary Kendall, Chapel Hill, NC

Sunday drive
  from Paris
to Giverny . . .
anticipation
half the delight

we stroll through
Monet's small village
the brilliance of greens
tints of lilac, silver
& old rose

his beloved home
full of color
& memories of children
playing, voices
long forgotten

all these years
together, your steps
in time with mine—
the unexpected scent
of old damask roses

stopping to study
fritillaries, tulips
& jonquils,
you reach out
& take my hand

soon we are adrift
in a huddle of lilac blue
stars of Agapanthus—
our lifetime together,
a flicker in time

wax and wane
Debbie Strange, Winnipeg, Canada

a tenderness
of snowdrops emerges
every spring
this temptation to fall
in love with you again

dandelion wishes
stolen by furtive winds
when you asked
for your freedom,
I promised to let go

wet cobbles
outside the flower shop
fallen petals
have pasted a rainbow
to this dirty street

Arco Iris*
Amelia Fielden, Wollongong, Australia

kangaroo paw
blooms with scarlet curves
in the courtyard
where I drink a daily glass
of citrus sunshine

winter wattle
golden heralds of spring
lining the paths
to families playing
cricket on the park grass

this Tasman Sea
is never simply blue . . .
aquamarine
sapphire, cobalt, changing
with the hour and the sky

far distant
from rural dye vats
in Japan,
my indigo tablecloth
spread for hungry grandkids

growing wild
around old tree trunks,
how many
would it take to make
April Violets cologne

*Spanish for "rainbow"

Silent Retreat at New Camaldoli Hermitage Big Sur, California

Neal Whitman, Pacific Grove, CA

take heed—
when you empty your mind
you will clear out
debris of all kinds
as you let the tide flow

take heed—
when you sit long enough
you will notice
tall grass start to sway
in rhythm with the wind

take heed—
when you look skyward
you will see
cypress branches gently push
the sea mist inland

take heed—
when you take a deep breath
you will be aware
of being under and in cloud
your lungs filling with fog

take heed—
when you lick your lips
you will taste
essence of sea salt
and thirst to set sail

But That Was Long Ago
Elaine Dillof, Mystic, CT

is that the same guy—
Brooks Brothers tie
Hickey Freeman suit—
who nestled with me
under a blanket at Jones Beach?

forgetting to bring matches
and the franks
for the picnic grill
we bum a few from couples
in love like us

the scene in the film
I liked—
a man takes out an eye
rolls it across the floor—
he hated

these conversations
Bela Bartok or Beethoven
Marxism or capitalism
Crosby or Sinatra
getting to know him

about to split up
I say I'm hungry
and wet scrambled eggs
on hot buttered rolls
melt us together

at the Hubba-Hubba Diner
flipping through songs
on the table jukebox
we choose "Stardust"
of course

Remembrance
Herbert Shippey, Tifton, GA

books
on the shelf
gather dust
his chair on the porch
rocks in the wind

she keeps
the broken bowl
touches it sometimes
recalling
hands that held it

sheets flapping
on the clothesline
windows rattling
nothing on the road
but wind-blown leaves

Mirage
Minal Sarosh, Ahmedabad, India

will time
keep track of time?
railway station clock
his wave going further
and further away

wheat fields
the song he always
whistled
why didn't she recognise
love when it came?

reflection
a bridge under a bridge
the memories
she was still holding
also holding her

An Immigrant in the Homeland of Dreams
Chen-ou Liu, Ajax, Canada

beads of sweat
dripping from his forehead
my father
takes another smoke break . . .
in my dream loop he comes alive

one night I'm in Ajax
the next I'm in Taipei . . .
these leaps
of time, space and language
across this life-dream expanse

Family Legacy

Mel Goldberg, San Nicholas de Ibarra, Mexico

from my mouth
I hear
my father's voice
and wonder
who I have become

a discussion with
my younger brother
how differently
we remember
our childhood

still writing
about my father
thirty years after his death
I will never finish
saying goodbye

grandmother's mirror locket
once held father's photo
empty now,
just my face
in the mirror

The fourth tanka first appeared in TSA's 2022 anthology, *One Moment at a Time.*
—Editor

Numen
Jenny Ward Angyal, Gibsonville, NC

wingless
I beg the red velvet "ant"
to be my muse
together we'll hunt
for our true names

retreating
under the willow
I hum
an invocation
without words

no answer comes
but the sound of rain
sinking
deep into the humus
that I am

Ribbons
Claire Everett, Northallerton, England

this spring overture
is surely the work of a child —
song thrush
up and down the xylophone
greenfinch on kazoo

an infant's first word
takes shape in her mouth
and the world is new . . .
returning swallows
ribbon the sky

Scent of Jasmine
Margaret Chula, Portland, OR

I want to sit
on a hillside of tall grasses
and write poems
while you stand at your easel
and paint the clouds

rereading
a month's worth of poems
smiling, crying
you come to me
and hold my hand

all day
moving further away from you
I watch the clouds—
in the back pasture
sheep twitch their ears

after the lightning
after the thunder
and torrential rain
sweet scent of jasmine
on the morning breeze

Hidden Treasures
Joanna Ashwell, Barnard Castle, UK

cardboard boxes
in the attic
our hidden treasures
the stuffed bear
no longer held

Wendy House
at the garden's end
my own space
to dream, to colour
childhood adventures

pen pot
holding so many
different colours
each day
a new sky

broken wings
made of glitter
upon the shore
a child's world
capsized

Artwork
Keitha Keyes, Sydney, Australia

at the end
of a long phone call
I discover
the doodles I drew . . .
do they mean anything?

a rare treat—
farm children mix up
a bucket of mud
to paint their pictures
on near-empty water tanks

Avian Antics
Sheila Sondik, Bellingham, WA

magpies outsmart
the scientists—
their mates
remove those pesky
radio transmitters

electric lights
turn on and off
as Siri responds
to an African gray parrot—
his owner makes him stop

eight tough puzzles
don't prevent a hungry crow
from freeing food locked
in a plexiglass box—will human
brainpower save life on earth?

The Beggar Takes *Kroner*
Gerry Jacobson, Canberra, Australia

rolling
through the cafes
of Stockholm
ham rolls . . . turkey rolls
cheese rolls . . . smoked salmon

traditional
lunch at Stüre Hof
lobster soup
smoked fishes . . . white wine
our baby eats the table cloth

candles burn
at basement tables
all around me
Swedish café babble
echoes off tiled walls

struggling
to learn a few words
of Swedish
how I'd love to speak
all the world's languages

five blonde women
with white wine and gossip
at the next table
a lone dark man
studies his smartphone

the bakery
just takes credit cards . . .
cashless society
but the beggar outside
only takes *kroner*

Happy Hour
Michael Ketchek, Rochester, NY

the way she appears
to have done nothing
with her hair
the zen master tosses a leaf
on the newly swept walk

the poem I wrote her
on a cocktail napkin
left on the bar
the ink slowly melting
into a spilled martini

Undertow
Bona Santos, Los Angeles, CA

seahorse mating dance
on the seagrass bed
one click away
a match awaits
on the dating app

molted crab shells
wash ashore
all those times
I have wasted
my second chances

a school of fish streams
past my face mask
sometimes
the truth
is right before our eyes

Responsive Tanka

Beacons
Samantha Sirimanne Hyde, Sydney, Australia
Marilyn Humbert, Sydney, Australia

vernal equinox . . .
on the garden archway
bursting wisteria
how quickly my spirits
soar to new heights

purple pennants
flapping high above
the crowd
cheering in the street
the football premier's parade

tropical drizzle . . .
clay lamp flames
wavering
under the shrine awning
white-clad devotees

sunstruck
the cathedral steeple
a beacon
calls choristers to practise
. . . the grace of music

high in the sky
these rainbow kites
floating
throughout the fest
squeals of delight

threads

Sanford Goldstein, Shibata-shi, Japan
Joy McCall, Norwich, England

unable
to find the energy
for tanka,
I still want to do strings
with my favorite person

those threads
between us
will hold
strong silk
blowing in the wind

at times
my own silk blown
in a Japanese wind,
may a few days this month
be even more windy

wild storms
batter my land
still, the strings
that hold us fast
do not break

our world
a together string,
we lean in wind or rain,
and still our string
endures

Reprinted with permission from *the last mile on the tanka road*, by Sanford Goldstein, a posthumous collection of tanka published in May 2023 by Stark Mountain Press.

into the world of books
Amrutha V. Prabhu, Bengaluru, India
Ryland Shengzhi Li, Arlinglon, VA

through my heart
a thrill of joy
as i sail on
a paper caught
inside word-waves

the sea foam kissing
my feet kissing
the sand . . . every bit
comes to life
in the pine-scented breeze

towering trees
bearing tempting fruits . . .
deeply rooted in my soul
a curious child peeks
into veins of every leaf

*putting down
another journal
with its yellowed pages
and unsteady letters . . .
autumn clear*

after day dies down
i clear the leftovers
from my plate
my life twists
inside out

*naked
before the crowd . . .
across the bookshop
a stranger picks up
my new collection*

bamboo
shrouded in moonlight
i am soaked
to the bone
in solitude

p.a. babusci

art: dawn m. robinson

Tanka Prose

Introduction

In the last issue of *Ribbons* I invited readers to reflect on the tanka prose that most appealed, or, as Theresa Cancro says, "stood out the most." Thank you so much to those who responded. I have sent your feedback to the individual writers, and they really appreciate your thoughtful analyses.

The tanka prose in the Winter 2023 issue of *Ribbons* that have captured the attention of some of our readers are:

"Visceral" by Gerry Jacobson
"Hush and Goodnight" by Michelle Brock
"It is always three o'clock in the morning" by Chen-ou Liu
"Timeless" by John Budan
"Bosque del Apache" by Ryland Shengzi Li
"Hoo knows" by Susan Burch
"Of Human Bondage" by Neena Singh
"Between Scylla and Charybdis" by Gail Brooks
"Finding Pearls" by Amelia Fielden
"Anchors Aweigh" by Richard Grahn
"Mother Mine" by Elaine Dillof
"My First Chess Set" by Ricardo J. Bogaert-Alvarez
"Electric" by Robert Erlandson
"Pilgrimage" by Marilyn Humbert

Perhaps the most important quality for any writer to consider is how to form a relationship with, a connection to, their readers. We want them to engage with our work in some meaningful way. For various reasons, these writers have achieved this connection.

Referring to "Bosque del Apache," Carole Harrison says, "I love this piece, so relevant, beautiful and thought provoking." And Joy McCall agrees: "He writes just what I feel, that there is a beauty and a kindness in nature that humanity so often lacks." Joy also has a strong connection to "Visceral" in relation to the shame she feels about the history of anti-Semitism in her hometown. And she loves

"Hoo knows," a humorous piece about not belonging. "Of Human Bondage" appeals to Carole for its delightful humour—"a light hearted tale with a serious centre." She also appreciates "Timeless" and "My First Chess Set," commenting that Ricardo's "Guess what?" within the prose is "the moment when the poet is now more engaged with the reader and the reader with the poet."

Gerry Jacobson's favourite is "It is always three o'clock in the morning." Calling it a masterpiece, he says, "it's haunting and meaningful and I love the innovative format." And Carole: "A short and powerful piece of self-reflection." The prose ends with one of my favourite last lines in the collection, "I hear Time passing in the sound of snow." The other is in "Mother Mine," a piece which Carole sees as "a sensual piece of writing, evoking the senses of sight, touch, and smell." The final phrase reads, "the lingering fragrance of the woman who was my mother's younger self."

It's interesting how readers have mentioned their appreciation of what could be called an aesthetic balance in a tanka prose.

Theresa Cancro's favourite in the collection is "Hush and Goodnight." She says, "It has the right amount of storytelling along with shifts among the tanka and prose that allow room for the reader to find layers of insight beyond the narrative;" and, in "Anchors Aweigh," Carole "loves how the two tanka snugly bookend the piece, and are richly beautiful in poetic image."

Could there be an emerging trend towards a preference for more than one tanka in a piece, especially if there is more than one paragraph in the prose?

To continue this discussion, I would like to give you another opportunity to express your thoughts. So, if there are any tanka prose here that you particularly like, for whatever reason, please write to me at tankaproseeditor@gmail.com with the subject heading "Tanka Prose Review." And I will forward your comments to the writers. Don't feel obliged to give a detailed review. A sentence is enough. Meanwhile, I hope you enjoy reading this collection.

—*Liz Lanigan*

Medicine Crow
Barbara Curnow, Canberra, Australia

As the sun retired, a shimmer of crows flew over my country home. And then, on my morning doorstep, a sliver of midnight; a crow feather, perfectly preened and as sleek as a slipstream. I placed it on my palm and imagined its twirling journey down through the final rays of day.

People speak of a "murder of crows." Perhaps to some, the long and languid cry conjures up remorse, or some dark deed or devilish intent.

But I welcome the song of the crow. It softens my soul and calls me deep inside, where loneliness and sorrow lie. And there it lingers, healing hurt and tending tender places that don't see the light of day.

As I listen to a crow call, it always seems to come from long ago and far away, and it takes me on a journey back in time. Melancholic memories surface to be felt and then released to fly. Pockets of nostalgia find a way to shine, and I feel the freedom of a heart restored and a mind of light and ease.

> she savours
> the soothing sounds
> of music . . .
> Bach, Beethoven
> and a sunset crow

Isabel
Joshua Michael Stewart, Ware, MA

We feed wild turkeys at the office. They strut down the sidewalk and stare at us through windows, their big eyes blinking. Their heads move with our movements, and they trot to meet us at the double doors when they see us get up from our chairs. We toss them bread, stale bagels, crackers, left over from the last staff meeting's cheese platter. A co-worker feeds them salted peanuts from a large jar she stashes in her desk drawer.

One hen we've named Isabel walks with a limp and has a messed-up wing. She's not plump like the others. Sometimes she's among the flock, but off to the side. Mostly, she comes alone. We try to feed her a little more than the rest. I'll make a separate bread-crumb pile and stand between her and the flock so she can eat peacefully. The gobblers puff their feathers and fan their tails but keep their distance.

Over the weekend, an arctic blast rips through the region, plummeting the temperature to life-threatening levels. Frostbite could set in within minutes. Pipes freeze. Car batteries die. I worry about the turkeys, especially Isabel. I know they'd huddle for warmth, but would they include her or push her aside?

Monday arrives. Sun blazes. The temperature jumps up forty degrees. I climb from my car to go into the office, and heading straight toward me is Isabel, her legs moving as fast as they can. She stops two feet in front of me, flaps her wings, and purrs. "C'mon, Isabel," I say as I walk to the front entrance. Her feet click on the sidewalk behind me.

> winter stars
> thinking of the friend
> I couldn't save
> from the storms that raged
> within her childhood home

Bullfrog in a Mayonnaise Jar
Margaret Chula, Portland, OR

In my dream, the bullfrog has grown so big its stomach presses right up against the side of the jar. A dank olive-green, its skin is wrinkled and pockmarked. Is it dead? No, it moves. The bullfrog has been living off its own body for a long time. It looks so ugly that I'm afraid to open the jar. Feeling sorry for it, I punch a hole in the lid to allow it to breathe. The frog shrinks itself to a size where it can wriggle out. I watch it struggle. I cannot help it now.

> months after
> bariatric surgery
> she's still hungry —
> the long, thin scar
> just beginning to fade

Phantoms
C. William Hinderliter, Phoenix, AZ

It is June in Phoenix, and as I look out my living room window, the image of a bedraggled stray cat catches my attention. I know this cat, and in a moment of sympathy, I decide that I should get it some water. Since it is only 104 degrees, and I am wearing socks, I don't bother to put on my shoes before I go outside.

When I approach the cat, it gets up and moves away from me . . . and waits. So I follow. Then it moves and waits, and I follow—a pattern reminiscent of trying to catch pigeons as a small boy.

Intent on my purpose, I barely notice that I've followed it down the street, up my neighbor's concrete drive and onto his porch, before it suddenly jumps behind a bush.

Thwarted, I pitch the water on the lawn and start my journey home. While walking, I notice that the hot concrete has gotten really hot . . . really, really hot. I hot-foot it home as quickly as I can, but burn off several layers of skin in the process.

Time passes, and the burns get infected . . . then the infection gets septic, then . . . seven surgeries later, I am lopsided.

And I still can't escape the irony of the fact that I didn't even *like* that cat.

Gone now are the feeding tube, IV, and oxygen tube. But I still feel my missing legs . . . until I look down, and they suddenly disappear.

> reality
> punches me in the gut
> recovering
> I dream of dancing
> on my ghost feet

To Dance with Another
Gerry Jacobson, Canberra, Australia

    when you move
    and stretch towards
    a still point
    and sense the breeze
    on that hot body

Socially distanced, we dance alone but with awareness of our partner's energy and rhythms. How is my movement influenced by hers? So I'm the dancer, and the observer, and I'm dancing with a partner. She's at floor level; I'm standing. Observing her left leg move, I become aware that my left leg "needs" to move.

    feeling
    the restless energy
    of another . . .
    am I supported?
    am I constrained?

We explore the unseen relationships and the "sixth sense": proprioception. How do our bodies, our cells, respond to what's going on around us? Seeing her movement, I respond with my own dance. Then I turn away and respond to how I sense she's moving. There is no choreography; a watcher tells us it's beautiful.

    rain drops
    patter the roof . . .
    observing
    my racing thoughts
    my mindless movement

Spirit of the Forest
Theresa A. Cancro, Wilmington, DE

If fairies really exist, where do they frolic? That new burrow under the tulip tree's roots, does it lead to a miniature dance hall where they waltz at the cusp of dawn to the warble of white-eyed vireos and the beat of soft rain?

>the scent
>of intoxicating trumpet flowers . . .
>while mortals slumber
>Titania and Oberon twirl
>under a haloed moon

A murmur we can barely hear, they're just out of reach, the old souls of the woods, faint impressions of sprites lilting through deep moss — teal, brown and shimmer, twined together in the heart of bent oaks.

>during a hike
>off the beaten path
>I glimpse the green man . . .
>he opens his eyes,
>tilts his head and smiles

Coming Around Again
Adelaide B. Shaw, Somers, NY

The heads down. The heads up. In tight bud. In full bloom. Golden yellow and bright white. And, some orange. Daffodils. What I see as I drive on twisting roads. A single clump here. A dozen or more someplace else. Neat displays, organized and obviously planned. Wild displays along the road. Nature's quixotic hand. Small houses and mansions. Farm houses and barnyards. A few days ago, nothing to see, but today . . .

the wait
may be hard or easy
fast or slow
spring comes in dribbles and drops
or in an explosion

After the Storm
Ryland Shengzhi Li, Arlington, VA

cloudburst
the roads, rivers
going home now
my feet in wild water
broken blooms

As suddenly as it came, it went.

My sneakers, though, are still soaked. So I put on dress shoes for this evening's walk. Now every step feels different, more tender, careful, as though the sidewalk were a mass of petals just shaken free.

The world seems clearer. The streets are rid of their facade of gold-green pollen, gold-brown dust. My heart, are you also clearer?

yaezakura*
along the median strip
a star-of-bethlehem
stands alone
thin, split petals

I am tired. My feet pause: a tulip tree is just beginning to bloom, its young leaves bowed with raindrops.

The birds, though, do not tire. They call and call: song sparrow, house sparrow, wren, robin, cardinal, on and on.

spring dusk
lingering a while
in the high trees
mockingbirds sing
a daydream

*Multi-layered cherry blossoms or those with more than five petals.

Following in His Own Footsteps
Richard Grahn, Evanston, IL

he tends his dreams
'til the break of dawn . . .
songbirds
gathering in the field
signal it's time to harvest

Here, beneath the clouds, a boy feels the first drops of sky dripping from the leaves. Soon he's a walking sponge, the trail oozing around his soles. A humming patter lulls the forest to sleep. He pauses at the top of a rise, the valley below frozen in time like an Ansel Adams photograph.

damp moss
blankets a rotting log . . .
time perfumes the air
with the sweet scent of death
feeding life

He takes the long way home. But when he gets there, he just keeps walking—walking into the sunset.

        many paths traveled . . .
        the pilgrim
        follows a dove
        as if it could carry
        a mountain

Fifty years later, on another rainy day, he pulls out a weathered memory, and like a muddy shoe, begins to clean it off. He feels drenched cotton clinging to his skin, sees a shaft of sunlight poking through the clouds, hears a chipmunk chirp. A doe and fawn bound across the trail. Then out comes a rainbow that tells him to move on.

        repurposing
        toybox relics—
        viewing the moon
        through his kaleidoscope
        he finds a field of stars

when nature calls thee to be gone
Alan Peat, Biddulph, UK

She rings and sounds happy; says she'd read through the notes they'd left and had come to the conclusion that a drink would be out of the question, but the weekend nurse had just called and thought that a couple of glasses would be OK . . . as long as she doesn't overdo it.

So we meet at the old coaching inn and at the end of the evening agree that we'll do it again, on one of her good days.

        all four of us
        at sea, red-eyed
        by a late night fire
        more glow
        than flame

Still, a Quickening
Mary Frederick Ahearn, South Coventry, PA

Another April, the month when, for some, desire overtakes memory, even if only in small measure. Winter's deep dreams of green places, smells, and birdsong become real for at least another spring. I remember when and where to look for the bluest of the muscari, down by Pigeon Creek, and rejoice when they are there in the cool grass this year again. Over in Warwick, along another creek, the most vivid of all greens are the skunk cabbages, their scent more a pleasure than not. Trout lilies with their mottled leaves and sun-gold petals grow near wide swales of spring beauties and violets. All these, ephemeral and precious, are increasingly scarce. Mother taught me about them, where to find them, their names; and her mother taught her. Some I haven't seen in many springs. Where is the wild ginger, trillium, trailing arbutus? Maybe next spring . . .

> silver hair
> worn long and loose again
> shining in the sun
> an old woman by most defined
> walks in the fields another spring
>
> on the trees
> young, tender-green leaves
> overtake the blossoms
> which fly away, fall away
> in the natural order of things

dreamscape
A A Marcoff, Leatherhead, England

an egret comes straight out of a dream its nature its quality is of dreaming itself into being with the light and the white of its wings opening like a Japanese fan as its magic casts a spell upon the water like a moment of snow flowing on the white wind I no longer know whether it is my waking mind that grasps this reality of a bird in flight or whether I too am always in a dream when I behold its light in the simplicity of the beauty of a morning seeing a grace of air and breeze as it glides over the river becoming the reality of dreams and when dawn breaks over the valley it will be time for consciousness and sun to become one great dream in the sky of existence

> an egret
> glides over the river
> in another dream
> I might have been
> its wings

If Pigs Could Fly
Michael Lester, Los Angeles, CA

"Let the rain fall!" he exclaims—as if he could do something about it—his arms outstretched like a human biplane; his lips moving like a stuttering propeller; the rain tumbling down in thick, pelting sheets with such force it splatters high onto his pants' legs. James has been a daredevil from birth it seems, carrying the scars of a thousand lost battles on his battered body. It's been a tough year for him, what with the divorce, the premature death of his only son, the failure of his latest reckless business venture, and the unexpected and unpleasant diagnosis of an aggressive, inoperable tumor in his right lung. The view of the ocean and the surrounding communities from the cliff are staggeringly beautiful on a cloudless day, but today he can't even see the rocky shoals at the base of the cliff.

> I will miss
> the exciting derring-do
> of my brother
> as he flies off the cliff
> into his last great adventure

Unfinished
Jackie Chou, Pico Rivera, CA

I start telling a friend about missing the person I was when I was a teen, about my undaunted spirit, my ability to accomplish things without inhibition. He suggests I was just naive back then.

>new moon
>an unfinished sentence
>dangles in the air
>I point to the navy sky
>changing the subject

As Big as Tom Thumb
Susan Burch, Hagerstown, MD

Two of my friends tell me they're going back to traditional writing & another, that my funny *senryu* just don't measure up. Add that to the tanka & tanka prose I write, which are already the ugly stepchildren, & I can't help but feel utterly alone & less than.

>hollow moon
>where does
>the last freak
>in the freak show
>go

Alienated
John Budan, Newberg, OR

I'd attended a university function where I'd met one of my heroes, Neil Armstrong. I can't wait to see my old friends and share my excitement. It's been ten years since I've seen them or visited my hometown. We meet up at a gentrified chain restaurant, which I do not recognize. The quaint old bars that served the famous Manitowoc fish fries are gone. When I begin to tell them about the astronaut, I am interrupted with "fake." They reveal that they do not believe that men actually landed on the moon. The conversation quickly switches to football, which I don't understand, something about the Green Bay Packers?

Was it Thomas Wolfe who wrote, "you can't go home again"?

> impending storm
> over rolling waves
> a bouncing tugboat
> enters the break wall
> of its home port

A Matter of Some Weight
Linda Conroy, Bellingham, WA

I see it now, in the front hall of my family home, the heavy thing that father kept out in the shed, a three-footed iron anvil, shaped to hold a shoe as a new sole or heel is attached. I see his hands, his hesitation, and the meticulous precision of his craft.

> dream while you work
> do what you love
> igniting joy
> with care in every step
> bring pleasure to this life

I feel the smooth, worn handle of the curved knife used to trim the sole to size. I smell the glue and watch tiny tacks tapped into place. Where did the anvil go between that childhood time, when he made magic, and its ordinary presence today?

Maybe mother lugged it in and dusted it once he was gone, wanting it nearby to prop her boots; or kept it as a stop to keep the door ajar. I was far from here then, honing my own skill.

It's a dense, uncomplicated tool, despite all it has done, and as I run my fingers on its blackened base, I think of weight; our three wills hardened over time. I know it's better kept in sight lest we become like him, whimsical yet clumsy as years pass.

despite our wish
to be unique
we carry generations' genes
old threads of history
bring us tumbling back

Anything new, is anything new?
Chen-ou Liu, Ajax, Canada

Another round of tech layoffs after tech layoffs. Unseasonably cold spring weather now grips the city.
   The food bank lineup curls around the street corner. This burden of silence between my former colleague, gazing at frost on the ground, and me, staring at the late afternoon sky.

trapped again
in this endless meantime . . .
my past is dying
yet a new life can't be born
in this Promised Land

In Real Time
Carol Raisfeld, Atlantic Beach, NY

Antique shopping, I see an iron clock, austere, yet ornate. Hundreds of years ago, could it have been designed to impress? With exposed handmade iron works in an open iron cage, it is fascinating to watch the slowly turning gears, and listen to the precise "tick-tock" and the clear chime of the bell when a small mallet strikes the hour. Cotter pins, wedges and a wooden handle to wind the spring-drive are visible. I feel like I'm looking into Da Vinci's notebook. Oh my, so expensive!
   Is it possible that the beautiful patina was recently applied in the shop around the corner?

evening drizzle
the rhythm of wiper blades
between sighs
a cricket under the seat
keeps perfect time

Heart and Soul
Ricardo J. Bogaert-Alvarez, Denver, CO

I'm driving in the left lane of the four-lane Speer Boulevard, Denver, rush hour. Suddenly the cars in front of me start moving to the right. As I follow them, I notice three cars stopped; the drivers standing side by side, looking at the ground. Then I see him lying face down on the street, blue jacket, blue jeans, brown boots, a pool of blood around his torso, red as a robin's breast. I continue driving. Three blocks ahead, the ambulance and firefighters are approaching the scene, sounding like the angels of apocalypse. I don't know if the guy is a jay walker or a drunk or a homeless man. It doesn't matter to me; that night I pray for his soul in my rosary.

may his heart
be lighter than the feather
of goddess Ma'at*
in our garden today
I see a robin

*In ancient Egypt, Ma'at was the goddess of truth, cosmic balance and justice. After death a body had to pass through the Hall of Judgment, where the heart was weighed on a scale against an ostrich feather, Ma'at's feather of truth. Only if the heart was equal to (or lighter than) the feather, could someone enter paradise.

Wide Stretch of One Ocean

Neal Whitman, Pacific Grove, CA

Point Lobos is a California State Natural Reserve nine miles south of our Pacific Grove home. My wife, Elaine, and I visit often to walk its trails. Binoculars around our necks, our well-worn quip is, "Yes, we are for the birds!" Almost always, we decline the offer of a docent to join a guided tour, but on this occasion, a volunteer, Wayne, seemed so welcoming we said, "Sure, we would love to," with us now making it a gaggle of seven sightseers. Wayne brought us to a promontory and, with his back to the ocean as we faced the waves crashing on the cliff below, he told us about the Tor House that the poet, Robinson Jeffers had built on Carmel Point where he could see Point Lobos. He had once remarked that, in the mist, it looked like an oriental landscape painting. Our docent then recited an excerpt from one of his poems, "Continent's End":

> I gazing at the boundaries of granite and spray,
> the established sea-marks, felt behind me
> mountain and plain, the immense breadth of the continent, before me
> the mass and doubled stretch of water.

As he was speaking, a great blue heron gently landed on the kelp in the bay behind him. Elaine softly said, "Wayne, slowly turn around. You have called in the spirit of Robinson Jeffers."

> we stand and look out
> before us a wide blue swell
> laps Japan's shores . . .
> is there someone over there
> thinking the same thing of us

Yuko's Fans

Amelia Fielden, Wollongong, Australia

>fluttering
>her blue Kyoto fan,
>Yuko glances
>round the respectful room,
>sighs a sensei's sigh

The sensei* never raised her voice. Whatever challenges arose in the Tower Society's monthly tanka workshops were handled serenely, and with the nuanced movements of her folding fan.

As a teacher of traditional Japanese poetry, Kawano Yuko most often wore kimono, with a seasonally accessorised fan tucked in the top of her obi. For her rare appearances in Western clothing, the fan was carried in a Gucci handbag, from which it was always the second article extracted after her spectacles.

A closed fan was pointed at the person whom she wished to speak next. It was tapped on the table once, to emphasize her point . . . two or three times, indicating *enough of that*. And sometimes, regardless of the temperature in the classroom, sensei would waft an opened fan to and fro across her face.

I had been designated Yuko's official translator. In the Japanese autumn of 2009 we met to work together for the last time. My beloved mentor was terminally ill. On parting, she presented me with one of her elegant fans. It has scarlet maple leaves painted on the palest green silk; too precious to use.

>husky-voiced
>fanning her flushed cheeks
>the poet speaks . . .
>my pen transforms her words
>for English posterity

*Sensei, literally meaning "before born," is the appellation given in Japan to one's superior, mentor, teacher, or an expert/specialist in any field, from tea ceremony, to medicine, to motor mechanics.

endearments
you cannot utter . . .
this cave
that never sees
one shaft of sun

Sanford Goldstein's Tanka World: Part 1
A Diary of the Emotional Changes in a Man's Life

Randy Brooks

Dr. Sanford Goldstein was born on December 1, 1925 and recently passed away on May 5, 2023. Therefore, it is an appropriate time to consider and celebrate his lifetime contributions to the literary art of tanka. Through his work as a translator, he made extensive contributions to our understanding of modernist Japanese tanka. However, for this essay, I will focus primarily on his contributions as a writer of tanka in English.

In the fall of 1975, my first semester as a graduate student at Purdue University, I met a quiet professor of creative writing who would become a significant influence and mentor for my life as a scholar, editor, teacher, and poet. His name was Sanford Goldstein, but everybody called him "Sandy." I'd often see him in the coffee shop in a booth by himself, writing poetry in a journal. If he was intensely spilling out poem after poem, I would leave him to his java muse, but sometimes, he would wave me over. We'd discuss his latest translation project, Zen Buddhism, news about poetry publications, or just talk about family. He was a member of a poetry writing group, mostly professors and local poets, which I joined as well. Soon I was studying modernist Japanese poetry and creative writing with Sandy. I would often bring my latest haiku or tanka attempts for him to bloody up with suggested edits. After a class that included writing tanka, some of his students—I was among them—formed a writing group focusing on tanka, senryu and haiku. At about this time my wife and I started publishing *High/Coo: A Quarterly of Short Poetry*. Sandy and several of the students were contributors.

Looking back, I think his most significant influence was his example of living the life of a poet. His discipline of daily writing about the emotional truths of his life, his integration of academic scholarship interests with his own creative work, his sharing work with others directly or through publication, and his humorous and encouraging approach to teaching made his life one worth emulating.

In Part 1 of this essay, I invite you to consider how his translations of leading modernist Japanese tanka writers helped shape his poetic goals for writing tanka in English. We will see how Goldstein developed his own minimalist approach and personal voice by keeping a lifelong diary, honestly recording the changes in his emotional life. While Sandy loved Japanese culture and lived in Japan much of his life, he avoided Japanese topics, language, and mannerisms. He knew that his tanka, even about Japanese experiences, came from a "gaijin," or outsider, perspective. I will share some of the best work from his published collections of tanka, which were often organized into strings of tanka on related topics. Part 2 will appear in the next issue of *Ribbons*.

I hope you enjoy this guided tour into Sandy Goldstein's world of tanka.

Modernist Japanese Tanka

Goldstein's interest in modernist Japanese poetry began at the start of his academic career. He earned a B.A. degree from Western Reserve University in 1948 and completed both M.A. and Ph.D. degrees from the University of Wisconsin. His first academic position was at Niigata University in Niigata, Japan, 1953–1955. Wanting to learn more about Japanese language, he studied at Stanford University, where his wife received an M.A. in anthropology. In 1956 he became a professor at Purdue, where he taught until he retired in 1992. During his years there, he received multiple Fulbright Fellowships at Niigata University, including the following years: 1964-1966, 1972-1974, 1980-1982, and 1987-1989. After retiring from Purdue, he went back to Japan and taught at Keiwagakuen Daigaku, a small college in Shibata, until 2005.

One of the most fortunate consequences of his years in Japan was his long-time translation partnership with Seishi Shinoda. In an essay on himself for *Simply Haiku* (2003), Sandy wrote: "Having come across some translated tanka of Takuboku Ishikawa in the early 1960s, I found tanka was the form I had been waiting for. And that began a period of thirty years or so of translating tanka with Professor Seishi Shinoda, my precious colleague at Niigata University." These translations of leading modernist Japanese tanka writers include: Akiko Yosano's *Tangled Hair* (1971); Ishikawa Takuboku's *Sad Toys* (1977); Takuboku's *Romaji Diary and Sad Toys* (1985); Mokichi Saitō's *Red Lights: Selected Tanka Sequences from Shakko* (1989); and Masaoka Shiki's *Songs from a Bamboo Village* (1998).

In an interview with Pamela Babusci, Goldstein tells why he was interested in translating and studying these Japanese masters. "Akiko was unusual as a woman's liberationist in Meiji Japan. Takuboku's colloquial, down-to-earthness made his appeal to me great. He suffered and suffered. I feel and can understand—as I can with most of the poets I translated. Mokichi Saitō was important to me because [through studying him] I realized what a true tanka sequence was . . . . Shiki's great suffering moved me. His life is itself a study in human courage. Shiki also wrote the first real sequences in Japanese. The variety of his subjects made him dear to me."

Translator's notes from the introductions to these books also indicate why Goldstein was attracted to modernist Japanese tanka. Shinoda and Goldstein refer to the tradition of Japanese court poets over the centuries and how they continued to emulate the poetry of the *Kokinshu*, published in 905. In the introduction to *Tangled Hair*, Shinoda and Goldstein discuss changes in tanka in the late nineteenth and early twentieth centuries. The ancient court tanka was still worshipped "but as time passed, many words and phrases were totally incomprehensible to the mass of readers. Those families versed in the art of tanka capitalized on the inscrutable expressions in these poems and monopolized the field. The prestige of the poetry families was heightened; moreover, the financial rewards were great. For hundreds of years the heirs of these families were initiated into the well-guarded techniques of the art. As a matter of course, poets and their poems were conservative in the extreme."

How did modernist Japanese poetics influence Goldstein's approach to writing tanka in English? He wanted to broaden the content of haiku beyond the beauty of nature and safeness of polite language, and he likewise sought less prescribed content and form for tanka in English. He admired Akiko Yosano's boldness of expression and new content of forbidden love. Goldstein summarizes his poetics in the introduction to his collection, *This Tanka World*: "Akiko's

Tangled Hair prepared me for tanka as love, Takuboku's *Sad Toys* for the broader spectrum of all man's activities. I think of myself, though, as Takubokian. It was Takuboku who brought tanka closest to colloquial language while still guarding its poetic element. Takuboku who said that the tanka need not restrict itself to thirty-one syllables, Takuboku who taught me that tanka is a diary of the emotional changes in a man's life. I feel my own tanka are non-confessional diary, and I am supported in this belief by one of my colleagues who calls my five-liners utterly personal and intimate but perfectly public."

In an article, "The Eye of Tanka," published in *Blithe Spirit* in 2012, Goldstein writes: "I have been on my tanka road for more than fifty years, so my eye has steadily been on tanka. That means of course that I write about myself, the thoughts and feelings I have, the people I meet, the images in front of me, the family or relatives or few life-long friends. The possibilities are immense. Tanka is perfectly adaptable in our culture or in other cultures in spite of its Japanese origin. But it is time to move on to the construction of tanka itself . . . . [Takuboku wrote the following in his] 'Poems to Eat,' printed in the *Tokyo Mainichi* newspaper which serialized it from November 30 to December 7, 1909: 'Poetry must not be what is usually called poetry. It must be an exact report, an honest diary, of the changes in a man's emotional life. Accordingly, it must be fragmentary; it must not have organization.' I have called myself Takubokian for decades. In another essay called 'Various Kinds of Tanka' (December 20, 1910), Takuboku wrote, 'As for the content [of tanka], we should sing about anything, disregarding the arbitrary restrictions which dictate that some subjects are not fit and will not make one. If only we do these things, tanka will not die as long as man holds dear the momentary impressions which flash across his mind, disappearing a moment later during his busy life'."

A Diary of a Man's Emotional Life

In the introduction to *This Tanka Whirl*, Goldstein writes: "I have always felt that Takuboku was right when he said in one of his essays that tanka is a diary of the emotional life of the poet. Throughout the years I have followed this principle, yet I have myself felt that the content of traditional tanka was too restricted. Poets talk about love, about nature, about death, about friends, about frustration, about mothers and illnesses and trips. And I have done that too. But I have tried to broaden even more the content of tanka—the games of children, the impossibility of the tanka form itself, the connection of tanka to literature, my Zen experience and tanka, a multiple diversity."

In an interview by Robert D. Wilson for *Simply Haiku* (2009), Goldstein explained his usual process of writing in his journal. Wilson asked: "What goes through your mind when composing a tanka, and how do you know when one is finished?" Goldstein said: "Nothing goes through my mind. I spill my tanka. Whatever flashes through it or whatever I see in front of me can turn into a spill. Or even something spoken . . . . I keep tanka journals, so I go through them, even older journals . . . . And when I come across a tanka I like, I always go over the tanka. Revising, adding, but usually the tanka keeps its basic form . . . . Though I say spill, I go over my poems many times before sending them out, especially those that are sequences or strings. I let the tanka spill. And after it is in my tanka diary, I check, say, at the end of a year, to see the good ones or possibly good ones. Usually, I write 3,000 tanka a year, though now I cannot get to my tanka cafe that easily—in the states I could sit at McDonald's for two hours and write, during my trips home once a year. When I go through my tanka diary for the year, I usually find, say, 300, that are good or can be made into good. Out of these 300, I choose ones I think I can send out. So out of all these, say 35 poems, I can send these to journals."

Let's take a look at key collections of Goldstein's tanka.

Goldstein, Sanford. *Tanka Left Behind 1968*.
Perryville, MD: Keibooks, 2015.

Although this collection is one of his last to be published, it comes from one of Goldstein's earliest tanka journals. It is a diary of "the most horrible summer of my life. We decided as a family to travel to New York and see my wife's brother who was suffering from multiple sclerosis . . . my wife had a sudden seizure and was then operated on. While she recuperated in the hospital on the second floor, my daughter Rachel fell from her bike and with a concussion was put on the third floor. As if each of these two events were not enough, I received a phone call that my father had died."

Written in Goldstein's characteristic minimalist style, these examples are from his summer 1968 diary of his emotional life. With the inclusion of many tanka from his journal, in chronological order, the author notes that *Tanka Left Behind 1968* reads like a novel. I will cite a few of these tanka, maintaining the chronology. (Please read from left to right before reading down.)

all at once
she hums a tune
to herself,
my wife
on her hospital bed

my kids
splashing in their
uncle's pool,
why tell them of their
mother sleeping still

a nurse
gives my wife tea
with a spoon,
how beautiful that
simple act of swallowing

my kid on her
third-floor hospital
bed
tries to remember
how she fell from a bike

drifting
asleep on her
hospital bed,
she repeats the days of the week
the months of the year

a sudden call
as if the pain was
not enough,
my father dying
in his house in Cleveland

I listen
to my wife trying
the Beethoven,
her head sways to the rhythm,
her hand tightly in mine

Although these tanka are from some of his earliest journals, they exhibit characteristics of his minimalist approach. They are direct in stating the situation and establishing a scene. They move between two parts, shifting from observation to implied internal states of being. In his essay, "The Eye of Tanka," Goldstein explains that his tanka "is a dramatic vehicle—that is, the first three lines give a problem or area of interest and the last two make some statement related to that problem, preferably indirectly." For example, the second tanka cited begins with an observation of "my kids/ splashing in their/ uncle's pool," which helps the reader imagine a scene. Then it shifts to an internal question, "why tell them of their/ mother sleeping still," which connects to the broader context of his wife in the hospital. We simultaneously see and feel the children's world and the father's or husband's world. These tanka are written with simple, direct, everyday language, resulting in emotional intensity.

Goldstein, Sanford. *Tanka Left Behind: Tanka from the Notebooks of Sanford Goldstein.* Perryville, MD: Keibooks, 2014.

soon
she will be gone
four years,
I will light a candle
and set it on an evening plate

all dressed up
in my Florida
tan
and no place
to go

at poolside
I listen
to the women
in the water
talk about their dead husbands

roof fixed
and the running
in the toilet stopped,
I listen for ghosts
in this empty house

confessions
over tuna,
my two girls
telling me
their junior high peccadilloes

In these examples from additional journals, we can see that Goldstein continued to emphasize a two-part tanka strategy with shifting emphasis from external observation to internal realizations. A diary of a man's changes in emotional life. The early loss of his wife was a constant sadness and yet, as we can see in the last example, he continued to be a caring father.

> Goldstein, Sanford. *Gaijin Aesthetics*.
> La Crosse, WI: Juniper Press, 1983.

In his essay, "This Elusive Tanka World" published by *Simply Haiku*, Goldstein explains that he was a student of Zen and loved the aesthetics of Japanese culture, but he was always a *gaijin*, an outsider. "My decades-long love-affair with tanka makes my views on tanka old-fashioned, certainly not bold. For more than a decade during that time I was a follower of Zen, more like an outsider as I went through the various steps with my wife. I never felt that a moment might come when stepping on a brick or thunder-struck by the words of a Zen master, I might achieve enlightenment, but I did learn that the world is co-causal, that every good brings forth its opposite, that every change is often a step backward, that no definition remains steady because the world is perpetually changing. No matter. Zazen continues and the koan continues and the Zen neophyte fails and still goes on." He enjoyed the quest but had no delusions of becoming a Zen master.

The introduction to *Gaijin Aesthetics* is clear: "For sixteen years I have been a writer of tanka, that Japanese poetic form traditionally spilled in one line and divided into syllables of 5-7-5-7-7. And for twenty-eight years I have been connected to Japan, whether living on her shores or in America . . . [but] the Japanese dub foreigners as outsiders, *gaijin*, pronounced *guy-gene*. [And] whether I am in Japan or not, the feeling of outsider-dom persists . . . . My own foreign-brand of tanka is spontaneous, though occasionally re-ordered, re-shaped, and yet the desire persists that, like a line out of a Western poem, my own single line will spring fully armed from the head of Zeus . . . . Whether above or below, inside or outside, in Japan or not, in them, in my tanka world, I feel an aesthetic, a line connected and disconnected, ordered and broken, but with a rhythm and color and touch lighting up the commonplace world of *sabi* or *wabi*, past or present, darkness or dawn, a host of cascading opposites."

where's the depth
in these five lines down?—
I walk
a seaside road;
I talk to self

in the bicycle basket
the crone
pushed up
the slope—
tonight's flower arrangement

the curve
in this tea ceremony
flower
tells me what's wrong
with my penny world

As you can see from these examples, Sandy wrote his tanka in Japan, but they are about the *gaijin*'s mind and perspectives. He is a guest of the culture. Curious. Appreciative, but in his own tanka world.

Goldstein, Sanford. *This Tanka World*.
West Lafayette, IN: Purdue Poets Cooperative, 1977.

Goldstein was working on this collection when I met him at Purdue, so it was formative in my conception of minimalist English-language tanka. I still consider it the best collection of his work. In *Simply Haiku* he discussed the book's publication: "Once I stumbled across tanka, I started writing them in the early sixties. I would send out my tanka and would get rejections. It seemed almost impossible for the tanka to gain a foothold. Haiku was the rage. Eventually small magazines, some at Purdue in the 70's, began publishing my tanka. In the 70's a small group of Purdue poets asked me to join them. I was hesitant since I had had no real success with my tanka, but a member of the group read several pages of my tanka and insisted I join. The group decided to publish its own members and chose my book first. Thus, my first tanka collection appeared in 1977, *This Tanka World*."

Goldstein organized his collection around themes or topics and labelled each section accordingly—as "This tanka world of kids and mates mothers and dads" or "This tanka world of coffee cups and tables," for example. Later he called these chains of related tanka "strings." I have included a variety of selections to show the range of topics and approaches in this collection.

"of kids and mates mothers and dads"

> all I saw
> was the hole
> in my kid's
> sock
> when she performed

In this tanka, we have a single parent's perspective. As I read it, he is there for his daughter's performance but bothered by not being able to keep up or attend to her needs, evident by the hole in her sock.

"of coffee cups and tables"

> even
> in this fourth
> wifeless summer
> I take my coffee
> with cream

Everyone has their own ways of dealing with grief and loss. In this tanka the narrator notes the passage of time and how things stay the same. The cream in his coffee and memories of summers with his wife add an extra touch of simple pleasure.

"of zen and the master"

> reminded
> again
> of impermanence—
> how thick this Sunday morning
> snow

This tanka begins with abstract Zen concepts and ends with a one-word thud of snow.

> this February
> light
> lengthens
> the day wrapped
> in a cloth of cranes

The days are growing longer and the light stays with us. A cloth of cranes would likely be an elegant silk cloth, perhaps a gift for his wife from his days in Japan. I've always loved this tanka.

"of sickness and hospitals and death"

> stripped
> jabbed
> wiped—
> my wife
> on a hospital bed

A memory or nightmare from his wife's illness and ultimate death. The indignity. This is a powerful use of three quick verbs in past tense, followed by the present scene of his wife "on a hospital bed."

> planting
> a white
> chrysanthemum
> in the hair
> of the dead one

Another powerful tanka, sharing a moment from his wife's death. A symbol of loyalty, honesty, love, sorrow. And an interesting choice of the word "planting" as if it will take root and grow. But, of course, it won't. The finality of the last line is also striking.

"of things"

> something
> lonely
> about an umbrella in rain
> two legs
> moving

After the loss of a loved one, such as a spouse, the survivor sees couples sharing their lives. This is a seeing of loneliness. Just two legs, moving. The lyrical expression comes from the opening lines "something/ lonely," which is very direct, as tanka can be. The rain contributes to the mood.

"of strangers loners and outside persons"

> wifeless
> in front
> of a white stove
> after a 5:30
> class

> loneliness
> piles up
> at midnight
> and sometimes
> spills over

His loneliness is real and felt in a variety of situations and ways. Sometimes it "spills over," late at night.

"of sex and love and marriage"

> lighting
> the memorial candle
> for my wife
> I put it
> on a white plate

Goldstein was Jewish and followed the traditions of grief, such as lighting a candle on the remembrance day for a loved one. The white plate seems pure and simple. A plate from the kitchen.

> that young skin
> should not be
> this fresh
> in the December
> light

This is a tanka of attraction and holding back. December light is an interesting, subdued light containing the shadows of winter.

"of various kinds of nothingness"

> they ask   home
> about the cooking   to this nothingness
> cleaning, kids   and upstairs
> of midnight   more
> not a word   of the same

Both of these tanka address others and home. In the first one "they ask" about the domestic stuff. How does he care for his children and himself? How does he manage the household chores? Then we get the reality punch—they don't ask about how he gets through midnight. He's on his own for those dark times. The second tanka could be an answer to the question "they" don't ask.

"of food"

> even my youngest
> knows
> something's wrong
> cleaned up
> her plate

The scene of this tanka is about a child cleaning up her plate without a fuss. The underlying current is the tension and anguish that the child has sensed. She seems to intuit: "Don't add to the grief. This is not the time to fuss about eating your green beans."

[Part 2 of this essay will appear in the next issue of *Ribbons*.]

* * *

To find out about opportunities to pay tribute to Sanford Goldstein, please refer to the "President's Message" in this issue. Also, TSA members, see "Tanka Hangout's Next Theme: Tributes" in this issue, a request for your tribute tanka.

For those wanting to read more by Goldstein, a bibliography of his work will appear in Part 2 of Randy Brooks's essay in the next *Ribbons*.

Meanwhile, Sanford Goldstein's new, posthumous collection of previously unpublished tanka, *the last mile on the tanka road*, (Stark Mountain Press, 140 pages) came out in May and is available from Amazon.com. It includes strings of responsive tanka written with Joy McCall; one of the strings appears on page 77 of this issue.

David Goldstein's eulogy for his father can be read on the TSA website at: https://www.tankasocietyofamerica.org/essays/sanford-m-goldstein-eulogy

—*Editor*

Book Reviews

Earthbound, An Aerial View through a Tanka Lens
Ginny Short

***Earthbound: Tanka Prose and Haibun,* Jenny Ward Angyal. Columbia, South Carolina: Windy Knoll Press, 2022. ISBN: 979-8-833359-52-5. 54 pages, 6 x 9 inches. Paperback, $5.99, Amazon.com.**

This chapbook-sized collection by North American poet Jenny Ward Angyal is part elegy, part exaltation. The author's love for the natural world shines through in every piece of tanka prose and haibun, and her thoughtful and sometimes startling imagery is a song that runs through the work, bringing the reader into her moving meditations on the state of the world.

Okay, spoiler alert: if you don't believe in climate change or Anthropocene extinctions, then this book might not be for you. But if you are on the fence about it or can't find the words to deal with it, then this book might give a voice to those passions and feelings. On a personal note, I appreciate a writer who gets her facts correct, especially when it comes to biology—a subject to which I've given my own life. Angyal gets that right, in my opinion, and that hits a note of honesty and integrity that is important to me.

Angyal is based in North Carolina. Her poems do evoke that Eastern world, and this evocation is fraught with emotion, from "blackberry vines/ encircl[ing]/ a hollow log" to "the cry/ of a mourning dove" in the pinewood. I think that Angyal thus charts her own path using poetry as waymarkers "through a darkening world." A sense of place seems to be important—even critical—to her trajectory.

My favorite poem in *Earthbound* is her tanka series, "Tipping Point," which opens the book. Angyal describes the heart-stopping love and anguish we feel as we watch the world tip closer to the brink of disaster.

Tipping Point

diving
into the cold depths
of fear . . .
until I remember
each wave is made of water

Gaia burning—
and yet
one dewdrop
magnifies the glory
of a beetle's burnished wing

my bequest
to the seventh generation
memories
of the deep green eden
your ancestors once knew

one by one
I drop these words
into a well—
bottomless,
brimming with stars

I would have liked to see a different term for earth than "Gaia," as I found that charming but expected; still it is a lovely sequence and the final tanka is riveting. This poem "brims" with hope. Yes, this is how so many of us feel—or want to feel—that we are speaking into empty space, only to find our voice is not lost in a black hole, but dropped serendipitously into a place filled with light. This mirrors the journey we are taken on, from poem to poem to poem, in this collection.

Earthbound takes us through Angyal's own passions and life story. From her own early steps in "The Threshold" as a young college student pondering the nature of reality, to her meditation on what her granddaughter might be dreaming in "Insight," to the moving and heartbreaking poems of her mother's illness and what this means to Angyal in "Bread of Life," *Earthbound* is really a celebration of life. This movement from infancy to age, from life to senescence is part of the backdrop as Angyal explores the sorrow she feels about the ecological crisis we find ourselves in.

I love the poem "Many Happy Returns": it is a little cocky, mixed with a little horror and a bit of resignation. She starts out this tanka prose poem as a "giddy" young woman celebrating the earth's 5,974th birthday with college friends. She explains, "My friends and I had just learned about Archbishop James Ussher, the 17th Century Primate of all Ireland who calculated the age of the earth based in part on the Biblical 'begats' from Adam to Solomon. He concluded that the Earth was created at about 6:00 p.m. on October 22 in the year 4004 B.C." From this rather cheeky and humorous beginning, she ends the poem as a mature woman saying:

> giddy again
> I cannot catch my breath . . .
> as time whirls
> on gargoyle wings
> I join the *danse macabre*

The title tanka prose poem, "Earthbound," was of particular interest to me. It was a bit surprising as it starts out with a dream of flying. Who among us has not had recurring dreams of flight? Who can't recall that utter sense of elation, of life? I personally mark the end of my childhood with the loss of those exhilarating dreams. Angyal writes, "Not since childhood have I flown on the wings of a dream. And yet . . .

> surrounded
> by a cloud of swallows
> on the wing
> I become invisible
> . . . I become sky

This reminds me that we *can* fly still, and I think on the clouds of birds I have seen and the remarkable sense of exhilaration they bring. This is what Angyal reminds us: we live on a beautiful, beautiful world. Whether we are young or old or in between, our identity with the earth is what binds us. Angyal brings that identity to bear, baring her heart in both anguish and delight.

Bouquets of Migrant Tales: *wildflowers*
Ginny Short

wildflowers by Hifsa Ashraf. Foreword by Dr. Afzal Kahn. Uxbridge, United Kingdom: Alba Publishing, 2021. ISBN: 978-1-912773-45-9. 107 pages, 5.8 x 8.3 inches, paperback. £12 / $16. To order: info@albapublishing.com

This book is a collection of haiku and tanka, in which the haiku speak with the voices of migrant children and tanka represent those of migrant mothers. By Hifsa Ashraf, a poet and activist living in Rawalpindi, Pakistan, *wildflowers* is written in both English and Urdu, the national language of Pakistan. Even if one can't read the Urdu poems, they are still beautiful to see. The haiku and tanka alternate throughout the book, as if the children and the mothers are singing a call and response. This is the sound and the feel of the book.

wildflowers has two potential "title" poems. Both are haiku that resonate with the emotion that Ashraf captures throughout this book.

> abandoned children
> around the barbed wire
> wildflowers

> finding roots
> in the foreign land
> wildflowers

Recall that these haiku represent the expression of the children in this schema, and this makes the interplay between the barbed wire and wildflowers both stark and startling, and sadly beautiful. This sort of chemistry is common throughout the book, with images of beauty dancing with those of tragedy.

> hollow tree trunk
> covered in lichen
> there once
> I scribbled the names
> of my lost children

The voices of these human beings, migrants who cross unimaginable seas and deserts and mountains, come through in these poems. They are filled with longing ("following/ a skein of geese/ my evening thoughts/ outreach the border/ of foreign skies"); irony ("rain puddle/ my teen child floats/ his paper boat/ folded from a brochure/ about clean water"); beauty ("plumes of smoke/ curl around . . ./ the half-opened roses"); and scenes of daily living ("berry picking/ mom's hands/ furl, unfurl").

There is a reflection, too, on the horror behind the reasons for some migrations, as in this duo, where one can imagine first the daughter speaking, then the mother:

> war debris
> among empty shells
> a broken doll

> war remains
> the broken pieces
> of a doll's house
> I gifted to my daughter
> to keep her doll safe

There are many word pictures in the collection that illustrate the many places, mechanisms and causes of migration. These causes include war, as in the above pair, but also hunger or famine, and hope for a better future.

> wheat stubbles
> in my family field
> turn into ashes
> the harvest moon
> and the sparrow fledglings

On the margins of these laments, the sadness of the women, the children, the hunger and the waiting. This poem sings to me of both the pain of the present and the warm memories of this mother's past.

> July afternoon
> a laborer mother sings
> time and again
> the songs of harvest
> to her hungry child

I am not sure that those of us who are not migrants can truly understand this life. But we can try. This series of poems aims to describe the experience of a world most of us can't imagine, one we need to try to imagine, for outside of experience, without imagination there is no empathy. The number of people that are torn from their homes across the world is staggering. As a resident of a border state, I work with immigrants all the time: some documented, some not, and their stories are as varied as their faces. Across the world, millions of people leave their homes for myriads of reasons, but inside these pages runs a common thread: women and children and their deep feelings around their loss of home, the separation of families and the hardships both of the journey and the arrival into a new world.

> yet another place
> we spend this dark night
> miles away
> still wandering, still searching
> for our lost dreams

> family home
> with fading laughter
> of my children
> once we played
> hide and seek there

    I was a bit puzzled with some of the language, but as Ashraf states in her bio, she is "a pioneer in her country for writing modern, Japanese-style micro-poetry in English," so it is easy to overlook the occasional odd choice of some words. It was a bit of a distraction, but only a bit, as so many of the poems were gorgeous.

    I was puzzled, too, with the foreword. I am one of those people who reads such things, and I could not understand the connection between the author of the foreword and the poetry, and I kept looking for that relationship. It was written by Dr. Afzal Khan, a member of British Parliament, and a migrant himself, at age 11, from Pakistan. While he states that the book is inspired by him, it seems strange to read only poems about women and children and I could not see the inspiration. He states that the book "presented me as a success story," and that struck me as peculiar as well. I did not find that the poems presented him at all, much less as a success story, nor did these poems "highlight what success can look like for a migrant." These were not poems of success, but of loss, longing and loneliness. Also, writers of forewords typically focus on the book's author, not on themselves. I would have liked to hear more about Ashraf instead. So, my advice is to read the poetry first. Then, if you choose, read the foreword afterwards. The poetry stands well without it.

    In any event, it is the voices and the humanity of these women and children who count here, and this is the movement and the wildness in this bouquet of wildflowers. Overall, this book is a fine read.

Lifetimes in the Veins
Jenny Ward Angyal

Returning: Tanka Sequences, **Michelle Hyatt and Jacob D. Salzer. Lulu, 2022. ISBN: 978-1-387-54637-4. 100 pages, 6 x 9 inches. Paperback, US $13.50 from Lulu.com.**

The theme of *Returning* is woven throughout this handsome volume, which is enhanced by five color photographs by the authors. Drawing on their intimate engagement with the sea- and landscapes of the Pacific Northwest and the forests of northeastern Ontario, Jacob D. Salzer and Michelle Hyatt have collaborated to create sixty-four pairs of responsive tanka that wind through the seasons of a year, beginning in autumn and continuing through summer until the year returns to fall. Each pair of poems is a kind of call-and-response, with one poet offering image and reflection, and the other poet returning a response. But the deepest meaning of *Returning* is to be found in the book's dedication to "Mother Earth & Our Ancestors." These tanka broaden the genre's reach beyond the merely human to explore what it means to return to the roots of our being. To distinguish the poets in this review, Michelle Hyatt's tanka will be in italics.

> lifetimes
> in the veins of my hands
> mother's stories
> moonlight gently reveals
> a leaf's skeleton

> *labyrinths . . .*
> *long strands*
> *in my braid*
> *I weave and wind*
> *through an old growth forest*

In the first tanka, the veins of the speaker's hands hold his mother's stories as well as his own—two lifetimes. But then, in the last lines, we see the skeletonized veins of a leaf. The identification between the speaker's veins and the leaf's veins suggests that "mother's stories" may include Mother Earth's stories—many lifetimes in many veins. The interweaving of the human with the rest of nature continues in the response tanka, which winds the speaker's braid around and through the tree limbs in the forest until they become as one.

Many of these poems look back into origins and past lifetimes, as well as forward into the unknown that awaits us at the end of each brief individual lifespan:

> where will
> my last breath
> take me?
> sea mist slowly rises
> into moonlight

> *in a dust cloud*
> *quiet footsteps*
> *approaching . . .*
> *I look through the eyes*
> *of a bison*

Salzer's poem likens his own last breath to sea mist rising, suggesting a return to our origins in the sea . . . but the mist rises into moonlight, creating a sense of mystery. In Hyatt's response, sea mist becomes earthly dust as the poem's speaker looks not into but *through* the eyes of a bison, her own individual consciousness melding with that of another species. Perhaps that is where our last breath will take us.

As autumn deepens into winter, the sense of identification with ancestors, both human and other, also deepens:

> *moose tracks*
> *through a northern forest*
> *scent of snow . . .*
> *Grandmother's silence*
> *grows deeper*

> sitting
> on a wooden bench
> my mother's presence
> in the damp cemetery
> Wolf Moon

In the first tanka we find only the tracks of the moose but sense its presence. "Grandmother" may be the speaker's human grandmother . . . or the forest . . . or Grandmother Earth. In Salzer's response, the forest becomes "a wooden bench" and the scent of snow becomes simply dampness, but the sense of the *presence* of the unseen remains. This time it is the speaker's human mother . . . or Earth Mother. And overhead the Wolf Moon reminds us of the unseen presence of still other fellow travelers on this planet.

The fellow travelers moving through these poems include not only wild things but also the creators of human culture:

> *into the mystic . . .*
> *your piano progression*
> *carrying me*
> *on the wings*
> *of a snowy owl*

> a time warp
> in grandpa's stream
> my reflection . . .
> the long journey
> of mountain rain

Piano music has the same power to emotionally transport the listener as "the wings/ of a snowy owl." In the response tanka, time is bent like light passing through water as the speaker's reflection in his grandfather's (life)stream blends with the seaward journey of "mountain rain." In each poem, the "human" and the "natural" are intimately melded together.

That intermingling continues as spring follows winter:

> a long pause
> in the conversation
> about grandma's death . . .
> the sound of wind
> between mountains

> *jasmine flowers*
> *opening gently*
> *a familiar song*
> *I can only hear*
> *when it rains*

In Salzer's poem, wind through a mountain pass joins a conversation about the passing of a human ancestor; in Hyatt's poem, both rain and flowers become part of a half-heard song.

> *pussy willows*
> *on a branch*
> *caught in the light*
> *how subtly you remind me*
> *time is but a vapour*

> golden mist
> hovering
> over Takhlakh Lake
> ancient legends echo
> in the call of a loon

In the first tanka, ephemeral light on pussy willows asks us to ponder the nature of time. What is it, really? Is anything "real" but the present moment? But in the response, we hear ancient legends echoing "in the call of a loon," here and now. Past and present, "human" and "natural" are deeply intertwined.

The ever-returning year moves into summer on the solstice:

Summer Solstice
I prepare an altar
beside the lake
lingering a little longer
with my shadow

cracks
in the old lighthouse
wrinkles in time . . .
a golden sun sinks
into darkness

The summer solstice is the hinge of the year, when the days begin to shorten, inviting us to linger with our shadows—personal, ancestral, natural. And time seems not so much linear as "wrinkled," folded on itself in the ever-returning cycles of day and night and season.

early summer morning
after the storm
a gentle tide . . .
dreams ebb and flow
in the call of a loon

created by nature
endings and beginnings . . .
a beach mandala
gradually dissolving
into the Mystery

The 10,000 things*—human dreams, a mandala of sand, the loon's call—return into the Mystery from which they arose. *Returning* is a poetic journey through the cycles of life and death, beginnings and endings. It is an exploration into our true nature and the lifetimes of stories told in our veins. Readers who join the voyage will travel in wonder, accompanied by two sensitive and reflective tanka poets.

*In Taoism, the myriad manifestations of the one underlying reality.

An Ancient Tradition with a Modern Twist
Peggy Hale Bilbro

pages from a tanka diary, **Pamela A. Babusci. Rochester, NY, 2022. ISBN: 979-8847-851-67-1. 89 pages, 5.5 x 8.5 inches. Paperback. To purchase a signed copy, contact the poet at moongate44@gmail.com.**

Pamela Babusci's most recent book of tanka is small in size, but it holds a profound depth of emotion. Her title, *pages from a tanka diary*, lets us know before we even open the book that it is intimate and confessional—a memoir. Indeed, as I read some of the poems, I felt as though I were reading from the private diary of the writer.

Antoinette Libro, in her excellent introduction to the book, points out that both tanka and the diary format derive from a centuries-old Japanese tradition of poetry: "Babusci's poetry extends many of the themes characteristic of that time, particularly the emphasis on love poems and the ephemeral nature of life, the pervasive use of the seasons, most especially flowers, as metaphors to express one's innermost feelings, and the melancholia which pervades the tanka literature." Libro's introduction offers a guide to the collection, indicating themes and predecessors to Babusci's work. It is well worth reading before delving into *pages from a tanka diary*.

This tanka collection is divided into six sections, titled: "another indigo evening," "stuck in a bell jar," "silent grace," "deepest shade of regret," "depth of my sins," and "wear me like raw silk." Babusci leads us through each of these sections taking us from trauma, infidelity, and loneliness, through the profound emotions experienced in illness, loss, and isolation, into a space of forgiveness, self-value, and love.

The first tanka of the book is one of despair and ennui, even when contemplating nature.

> dewdrops or raindrops
> is it of any consequence?
> at the end
> of existence
> we all evaporate

The poem is, as Libro points out, in the tradition of the ephemeral nature of existence as well as an indication of the melancholy the poet feels. But as we progress through the sections, we come with her to the final poem in her diary, one expressing the sanctity of love.

> can love be holy?
> i am your
> eucharist
> pure white
> & edible

That place of purity and joy is reached only through a process of forgiveness of others and of herself—this is the thought that connects the second and third sections, and that moves the reader forward in Babusci's journey. The final word of the second section is "unforgiveness," while the first word in the following section is "forgiveness." The juxtaposition of these two tanka reveals the difficulty of the poet's struggle.

> after steeping
> the white tea bowl
> turns dark brown
> the bitter taste
> of unforgiveness

> forgiveness
> isn't easy
> it's damn hard
> prayer flags in the wind
> tattered and frayed

Babusci expresses her struggles and her journey out of despair through a skillful weaving of color. She describes herself as existing in a "polychrome world/ i, a monochrome/ woman." She bemoans having missed the possibilities of a life filled with color due to her own inability to love and forgive herself.

> bereft among
> a myriad of cosmic colors
> realizing too late
> i should have loved myself
> unconditionally

However, Babusci's poetry returns again and again to images saturated with color, especially the many shades of blue. She writes of indigo evenings, wild bluets, blue waves of pain, turquoise waters, and a sapphire lotus. Red becomes the color of adultery, while white is a two-fold shade. In the earlier tanka she associates it with pain, but as the book progresses, white becomes the symbol of forgiveness, love, and purity. As I read it, perhaps this is because white light is the collection of all the colors in the prism.

The fourth section, "deepest shade of regret," chronicles infidelity, and loss after the pain of separation and divorce, and returns the poet to the monochrome world of her earlier poem.

However, the final two sections lead us out of that world as Babusci learns to forgive others as well as herself. This is where we find mother-of-pearl, turquoise waters, a "garnet moon/ over poppy fields," and the poet's "red-blossomed kimono."

In addition to the use of color, Babusci refers frequently to artists and writers she associates with the emotions she feels. Unlike the way "Matisse's/ paper-cut collages/ blend seamlessly," she tries "to piece/ together [her] brokenness." In the paintings of Hopper she finds her own sense of isolation.

> sometimes
> i am trapped inside
> a Hopper painting
> within subtle brushstrokes
> of loneliness

In another tanka the artist Modigliani's reclining nude echoes the growing sensuality of the poet's emotions. And finally, she finds self-knowledge in Georgia O'Keeffe's painting.

    O'Keeffe's flowers
    or female genitalia?
    staring
    at the *Red Canna*
    i am convinced

    Pamela Babusci has presented a moving collection of tanka in which she maintains the intimacy of diary confessions, while skillfully leading the reader through her journey from loss and despair, to self-discovery and forgiveness, and finally into the delight of new love. Her use of color and the tanka format, her references to artists, and her inclusion of everyday activities all lead the reader into a sharing of her intimate moments. These tanka are beautifully written, drawing on an ancient tradition while remaining deeply emotional and personal. *pages from a tanka diary* is a book to be savored like an intimate conversation with an old friend. It is a conversation I will treasure long after reading Babusci's tanka.

News and Announcements

New Tanka Journal

Pamela Babusci is starting a new, small-print tanka journal called *the art of tanka*, to be published twice a year. Each issue will be limited to eighty tanka, one tanka per poet so that, she writes, "I can publish a lot of poets while keeping the costs of printing and mailing down. I am looking to publish the highest quality of tanka from around the world."

If you wish to be on her email list, or if you have any questions, contact her at: moongate44@gmail.com.

how can we not
also feel the rhythm
of april rain
with drops all around us
dancing to their own tune

an'ya

Index of Contributors

Margi Abraham, 14, 34
Mary Frederick Ahearn, 14, 91
Rupa Anand, 36
Jenny Ward Angyal, 14, 69, 114, 121
an'ya, 14, 32, 130
Hifsa Ashraf, 117
Joanna Ashwell, 15, 71
Pamela A. Babusci, 80, 126
Peter Barker, 48
Kathleen Beavers, 47
Mona Bedi, 46
Maxianne Berger, 52
Jerome Berglund, 15
Sally Biggar, 15, 58
Peggy Hale Bilbro, 126
Elizabeth Black, 11
Steve Black, 53
C.W. Blackburn, 46
Ricardo J. Bogaert-Alvarez, 39, 96
Michelle Brock, 15, 33
Gail Brooks, 46
Randy Brooks, 15, 100
John Budan, 16, 37, 93
Susan Burch, 16, 46, 93
Pris Campbell, 16, 33
Theresa A. Cancro, 37, 87
Teri White Carns, 39
David Chandler, 16, 40
Ram Chandran, 41
Anette Chaney, 16
Jim Chessing, 17, 45
Jackie Chou, 17, 51, 93
Margaret Chula, 17, 70, 84
Marcyn Del Clements, 18, 57
Margaret Conley, 52

Linda Conroy, 17, 40, 94
Sophia Conway, 38
Jeanne Cook, 50
Christopher Costabile, 17
Tim Cremin, 18, 36
Barbara Curnow, 45, 83
Anne Louise Curran, 49
Mary Davila, 18, 41
Elaine Dillof, 65
Jack Douthitt, 18, 36
stacey dye, 18, 40
Robert Erlandson, 19, 39
Michael L. Evans, 33
Claire Everett, 19, 69
Amelia Fielden, 19, 63, 98
Michael Flanagan, 19
Marilyn Fleming, 4, 19, 45
Diane Funston, 54
William Scott Galasso, 20, 47
Denis Garrison, 8
Mark Gilbert, 55
John S. Gilbertson, 35
Mel Goldberg, 68
Sanford Goldstein, 6, 8, 77, 100
Richard Grahn, 89
David Greenwood, 56
Jennifer Gurney, 58
Ian Gwin, 34
James Haddad, 20
Johnnie Johnson Hafernik, 20, 35
Hazel Hall, 20, 60
Jon Hare, 20, 45
Charles Harmon, 21, 44
Carole Harrison, 21, 42
Michele L. Harvey, 21, 43

Marilyn Shoemaker Hazelton, 52
Betsy Hearne, 54
Janet Ruth Heller, 42
David Lee Hill, 21, 45
C. William Hinderliter, 49, 85
Ruth Holzer, 22, 44
Elinor Pihl Huggett, 10, 55
Marilyn Humbert, 22, 76
Michelle Hyatt, 121
Samantha Sirimanne Hyde, 76
Lakshmi Iyer, 35
Rick Jackofsky, 22, 56
Gerry Jacobson, 22, 73, 86
Roberta Beach Jacobson, 22, 48
Barbara Kaufmann, 44, 59
Mary Kendall, 61
William Kerr, 22
Michael Ketchek, 23, 74
Keitha Keyes, 11, 23
Roy Kindelberger, 23, 38
Mariko Kitakubo, 23, 43
Kathy Kituai, 23, 51
Nicholas Klacsanzky, 53
Mari Konno, 24, 41
Robert Kusch, 56
Don LaMure, 24, 38
Carole Glasser Langille, 58
Liz Lanigan, 81
Peter Larsen, 24, 38
Michael H. Lester, 24, 92
Ryland Shengzhi Li, 24, 34, 78, 88
kathryn liebowitz, 44
Chen-ou Liu, 25, 67, 95
Bob Loomis, 42
Janis Albright Lukstein, 25
Jeannie Lupton, 8, 48
Heather Lurie, 49
Anthony Lusardi, 55
Kathleen Caster Mace, 56

AA Marcoff, 57, 91
Richard L. Matta, 25, 50
Joy McCall, 25, 77
Jen Meader, 58
Lenard D. Moore, 25, 41
Genie Nakano, 26
Suraj Nanu, 26, 54
David F. Noble, 5, 26, 36
Jan O'Loughlin, 47
Debbie Olson, 50
Pravat Kumar Padhy, 34
Christa Pandey, 55
Curt Pawlisch, 37
Alan Peat, 51, 90
James B. Peters, 26, 54
Dru Philippou, 26, 53
Madhuri Pillai, 27, 35
Amrutha Prabhu, 78
Patricia Prime, 27, 40
Carol Raisfeld, 27, 37, 95
Kala Ramesh, 53
Bryan Rickert, 27, 43
Elaine Riddell, 27, 56
Edward J. Rielly, 28, 54
Raymond Ro, 39
Dawn Robinson, 80
Margaret Owen Ruckert, 55
Jacob D. Salzer, 121
Michael Sandler, 28
Bona M. Santos, 75
Sigrid Saradunn, 28
Minal Sarosh, 67
Barbara Sayre, 48
Bonnie J. Scherer, 37
Richa Sharma, 40
Don Sharp, Jr., 28, 46
Adelaide B. Shaw, 28, 48, 87
Herbert Shippey, 66
Ginny Short, 114, 117

Ken Slaughter, 12
Catherine Smith, 10, 29, 50
Sheila Sondik, 72
Srini, 53
Joshua St. Claire, 42
Kathryn J. Stevens, 42
Joshua Michael Stewart, 52, 83
Robert Stone, 43
Debbie Strange, 62, 99
Jane Stuart, 29, 47
Lesley Anne Swanson, 57
Margaret Tau, 39
Mark Teaford, 29, 57
Julie Thorndyke, 34
Xenia Tran, 29, 36
C.X. Turner, 39
Christine L. Villa, 5, 49
Susan Mary Wade, 30
Patricia Wakimoto, 30, 44
Mira Walker, 51
Jeffrey Walthall, 52
Joanne Watcyn-Jones, 30, 38
Susan Weaver, 4, 8, 30
Linda Weir, 57
Michael Dylan Welch, 6, 50
Neal Whitman, 30, 64, 97
Rodney Williams, 51
Kath Abela Wilson, 31, 41
Simon Wilson, 47
Robert Witmer, 49
Wai Mei Wong, 43
Sharon Lynne Yee, 35
Beatrice Yell, 31
Aya Yuhki, 33

Submission Guidelines

Submissions to *Ribbons* are open to TSA members and non-members alike. Please include your name, as you wish it to appear, and your location (city, state/province, country) with your work. *Ribbons* submission deadlines are in-hand no later than

>April 30: Spring/Summer Issue
>August 31: Fall Issue
>December 31: Winter Issue

Ribbons editors will respond to all submissions within one month of the submission deadline.

Submissions must not be under consideration elsewhere, submitted to any contest, or previously published anywhere, including online; but tanka posted to online workshop lists or on Facebook are permissible. All rights revert to authors upon publication, except that the TSA reserves the right to reprint content from its publications on TSA social media sites and its website.

Ribbons seeks fresh material of the highest standard. Any tanka with a sensibility that distinguishes the form will be considered. Therefore, we welcome different syllable counts, varying individual styles and techniques, and diverse yet appropriate subject material. We also accept essays and interviews that offer fresh insights and information. As our space for essays/interviews is limited, you may query the editor with a summary before writing in full.

Tanka: For each issue, you may submit up to ten unpublished, original tanka *or* two tanka sequences (not more than six tanka per sequence) *or* one tanka sequence and up to five tanka. From among these, one individual tanka or a sequence may be selected. We prefer e-mail submissions, using the subject heading "*Ribbons* Submission." Send to: RibbonsEditor@gmail.com. You may also submit by mail:

>Susan Weaver, *Ribbons* Editor
>127 N. 10th St., Allentown, PA 18102

Tanka Prose: Please send one tanka prose piece to Liz Lanigan, our tanka prose editor, at TankaProseEditor@gmail.com. Please put "*Ribbons* Submission" in the subject line. The prose should not exceed 300 words. The number of tanka is flexible (within reason and when in service to the whole). Please include a creative title.

While submissions by e-mail are preferred, you may also submit tanka prose by postal mail:

>Liz Lanigan, *Ribbons* Tanka Prose Editor
>38 McClure Street, EVATT ACT 2617, Australia

Book Reviews: Please query *Ribbons* editor, Susan Weaver, (at RibbonsEditor@gmail.com), before sending your book for review.

Tanka Hangout: TSA members (only) are invited to send one original, unpublished tanka on the assigned prompt to our Tanka Hangout editor, Ken Slaughter, at tsahangout@outlook.com, with the subject heading "Tanka Hangout." He will acknowledge all email submissions, and if your poem is among the sixty to ninety selected for publication, he will notify you within a month after the submission deadline. Beneath the poem, please include your full name as you wish it to appear, followed by your town or city of residence and its location (state/province and country).

Email is preferred, but you may also submit by postal mail:

>Ken Slaughter, Tanka Hangout Editor
>24 Briarwood Circle, Worcester, MA 01606

Restrictions are few, and almost any treatment of the tanka form is acceptable, but please submit your best effort. The tanka will be read for thematic content, the depth and layering of meaning (often called "dreaming room"), vivid imagery, and suggested emotion. Any comments with your submission may also be considered, in part or in full, for publication. But please be sure your tanka does not rely on these comments.

For further guidelines, please refer to the Tanka Hangout in this issue or to the TSA website.

Made in the USA
Middletown, DE
03 July 2023